THE FOSSIL FACTORY

THE FOSSIL FACTORY

A Kid's Guide to Digging Up Dinosaurs, Exploring Evolution, and Finding Fossils

Niles, Douglas, and Gregory Eldredge

Illustrations by True Kelley and Steve Lindblom

Addison-Wesley Publishing Company, Inc.
Reading, Massachusetts   Menlo Park, California   New York
Don Mills, Ontario   Wokingham, England   Amsterdam   Bonn
Sydney   Singapore   Tokyo   Madrid   San Juan

Library of Congress Cataloging-in-Publication Data

Eldredge. Niles.

The fossil factory: a kid's guide to digging up dinosaurs, exploring evolution, and finding fossils / Niles, Douglas, and Gregory Eldredge; illustrations by True Kelley and Steve Lindblom.

p. cm.

Includes index.

Summary: Describes fossils, how to collect them, and what they reveal about dinosaurs and other creatures that inhabited the earth millions of years ago.

ISBN 0-201-18599-7

1. Paleontology—Juvenile literature.
2. Dinosaurs—Juvenile literature. 1. Paleontology.
2. Dinosaurs. I. Eldredge, Douglas. II. Eldredge, Gregory. III. Kelley, True, ill. IV. Lindblom. Steven. ill. V. Title.
QE714.5.E55 1989 560—dc20 89-6548

Cover illustration © by True Kelley and Steve Lindblom
Text design by Alison Kennedy
Set in 11½-point Century Expanded by DEKR Corp., Woburn, MA

BCDEF-VB-93210
Second Printing, June 1990

Many of the designations used by manufacturers and sellers to distinguish their products are claimed as trademarks. Where those designations appear in this book and Addison-Wesley was aware of a trademark claim, the designations have been printed in initial capital letters (e.g., Fred Flintstone).

Whether you are outside hunting fossils or doing activities at home, always obey safety rules! Neither the Publisher nor the Author shall be liable for any damage which may be caused or sustained as a result of the conduct of any of the activities in this book.

For Lara and Christopher,
Christopher and Michaela, and Matthew —
young paleontologists and great kids

Contents

Dig In!

How many fossils are there? Billions of them, filling up rocks all over the world. We tend to think that fossils are rare, and that only professional *paleontologists* (people who study ancient life) know enough to find them. But that's not true. You can find fossils yourself.

What's the first thing you think of when we say "fossil?" Dinosaur bones? That's probably true for most kids, and we have plenty to say about dinosaurs. But fossils come from strange sea creatures too, and from grains of pollen, and even from ancient humans. Fossils are any remains of ancient plants and animals — their bones and teeth, or their shells, or their woody stems. Or just their footprints. This book talks about them all.

Many fossils have turned to stone, or become *petrified*. (Or is it people who go to horror movies who are petrified?) Your teeth and bones are really stones already. They are made of a chemical called *calcium phosphate*, which is also found in nature as the mineral *apatite* (not appetite — that tells you when it's time for dinner).

Because bones and teeth are already made of minerals, they turn to fossils, or *fossilize*, easily. So do other things such as corals and the shells of clams, snails, oysters, and crabs. But first they must be buried before they break up and decay. Minerals may seep into them — *petrification* — making them tougher as the ages roll by. But most of all, they must not be attacked by acids in the soil or rocks that could dissolve them.

Most living things don't get fossilized. And most fossils will never be found. Still, fossils are a record of life, a kind of unwritten history. Because the pieces are all jumbled up and so many are missing, you could think of the fossil record as being like a jigsaw puzzle. Or maybe fossils are more like the individual pictures that are strung together to make a movie. Even if you don't have all the pictures in front of you, you can probably still get a good idea of the story by looking carefully at what you do have.

This book will tell you about fossils and fossil collecting, and, even better, it will show you how to use fossils to learn what life was like millions of years before you were born. What would it be like to bump into a *Tyrannosaurus?* How would you like to come across a dragonfly with wings almost 30 inches (75 cm) wide, or a centipede 20 feet (6 m) long? Can you imagine a fish getting up and walking to the next puddle? Then read on. Fossils have some pretty interesting stories to tell.

How Animals Disappear

A multiple choice quiz!

When animals die, they:
  A stop moving
  B fall down
  C decay
  D sink into the mud and are buried

Any of these answers could be correct, even the silly ones. But the answer that works best for forming fossils is D, sink into the mud.

Unfortunately for fossil collectors, most animals and plants simply C, decay. Bacteria and fungi are the culprits. Over many years they can completely consume an animal's body — even a whale — until nothing is left.

A covering of dry dust or ash may protect an animal so that its bones can petrify. In very dry deserts that don't easily support bacteria (or any other life) decay is very slow. In such "clean" places we can find dinosaur "mummies" — skin and all. But most animal remains disappear long before they can fossilize.

A Grave Matter

Try this experiment to see what can happen on the way to becoming (or not becoming) a fossil. You'll see how bacteria, water (both running and freezing), and other animals — the living, hungry kind — can change your "future fossils."

You will need
- a small digging tool (trowel or spade)
- a raw egg
- a big beef bone from the butcher shop or grocery store
- a piece of beef or chicken, left over from the dinner table, that has both meat and bone
- an apple
- a piece of cotton cloth, like a sock, a rag, or a scrap of cotton underwear
  (All of these things come from animals or plants. Add some more remains from living things if you want.)
- water

1 Dig a hole six inches (15 cm) deep for each item.

2 Place one item in each hole, cover it with dirt, and dampen the earth with some water.

3 Put a marker over each hole so you can find it again.

4 Check your burial sites from time to time to see if you've been visited by grave robbers. Has anything disturbed your markers?

5 Come back one month later and dig up your treasures. Did they survive? Did they change?

Hard Rock, Soft Rock

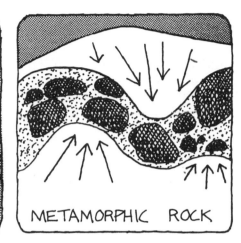

New rocks are made by volcanoes spewing out the fiery, molten lava from down below. Powerful forces inside the earth can change the rock. Wind and water can change it still more. New rock can even be made when sand just sits in one place — for millions of years. These processes give us three kinds of rock, but only one is good for fossils. Guess which one it is.

Igneous Rock

"Igneous" means "fiery." This is rock that comes red-hot from the oven, spewing up from deep inside the earth in volcanic eruptions. Igneous rocks, such as granite and basalt, were once actually liquid. Sometimes you can even see bubbles left over from where the rock was boiling. It's awfully hot down there!

Sedimentary Rock

This is rock formed from tiny grains of smashed-up and ground-up rock, or from broken and ground-up shells. The grains were usually floating in water. Then they settled to the bottom and built up in layers that hardened into solid rock again. Limestone, made from ground-up seashells, is one example of sedimentary rock.

Metamorphic Rock

This is igneous or sedimentary rock that has been smashed and cooked and rearranged by the heat and pressure of movements in the earth. All that cooking and crunching is pretty tough to go through, and it makes a tough kind of rock. Marble is one kind of metamorphic rock.

So which rock would you choose for fossil hunting? (Here's a hint: you'd have no luck at all looking in granite or marble, but with limestone you could strike it rich.)

Answer: Sedimentary

Making a Good Impression

Very often the fossils we find are not parts of the animal itself but a *mold* or impression its body left behind. A dinosaur footprint is one exciting kind of mold fossil from millions of years ago. A very important part of the human fossil record is some footprints a family left in an African mud puddle 3½ million years ago.

For molded fossils like this to be found, the impression has to be in one kind of mud, and the sediments that bury it have to be of another kind. That way, when the water dries out and the whole caboodle turns to rock, a crack will occur at the level of the footprint.

But footprints aren't the only impressions left behind. One of the most famous fossils of all — the first evidence of the evolution of birds — came from German limestone about 170 million years old. The earliest of the early birds died, sank beneath the water, and was buried in sediments. Its fossil bones were found along with a mold of its outside. The limestone had to be very fine indeed to capture the impression of a single feather.

Sometimes, after bones and shells decay to leave a mold behind, that mold is filled with minerals carried by water seeping through the rock. That sort of fossil is called a *cast*. Paleontologists have even found cast fossils made of silver!

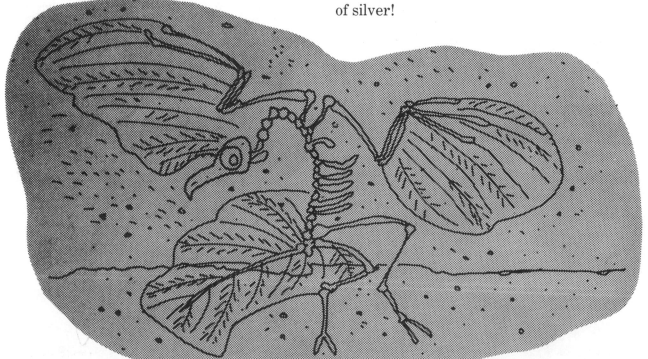

Cast Party

You can make your own plaster casts and molds. This way you can preserve the impression of a seashell, or a coin, or even a footprint.

You will need
- modeling clay
- plaster of Paris
- water (for mixing the plaster)
- a spoon
- an old plastic bucket or food container
- a knife
- scissors
- cardboard
- tape
- shampoo or cooking oil

1   Shape a hunk of modeling clay into a round slab, like a thick pancake. Talk a friend — or your puppy, or yourself — into leaving a footprint in the clay.

2   With the scissors, cut a strip of cardboard about two inches (5 cm) wide and long enough to go all the way around the edge of the clay. Wrap the cardboard around the clay and tape it tightly in place.

3   Mix a small portion of the plaster of Paris in the plastic container (follow the direc- tions on the package). Work quickly; it dries fast.

4   Spoon the plaster over the footprint until it is about an inch thick. Let the plaster harden for about three hours. Then gently untape the cardboard and peel off the clay. Set the plaster aside and let it get even harder overnight. You now have a plaster cast of the footprint.

5   Tape the cardboard around the cast so it fits snugly.

6   Brush the surface of the cast with a thin layer of shampoo or cooking oil. Make sure you don't miss any spots, or your plaster pieces will stick together.

7   Mix a fresh batch of plaster and cover the cast up to the top of the cardboard. Let the plaster harden for a day. Then tear away the cardboard and separate the two plaster layers. Let the plaster harden for another couple of days, and then rinse it off.

You now have a plaster mold and a plaster cast of the footprint. They should make a perfect fit.

Out in the Field

Here's how North America looks today from a paleontologist's point of view. As you can see, there are fossils to be found almost everywhere on the continent.

Imagine, for instance, that you're in Kansas, near the middle of the country. A few million years ago you might have been a little chilly: you wouldn't have been far from a glacier. A few hundreds of millions of years ago, your feet would have been very wet: the whole area was covered with seawater. (We'll explain this later.) But now, you're in a paleontologist's dream!

It's easy to find fossils sticking out from exposed rocks in Kansas, and in most of the rest of the country. Some places are better than others, but in this book we have collecting projects for you no matter where you live, as well as specific directions to sites near you. Almost anyone can catch and collect mysterious ancient animals with names like brachiopods, bryozoans, echinoderms, and trilobites (plus more familiar guys such as clams and snails).

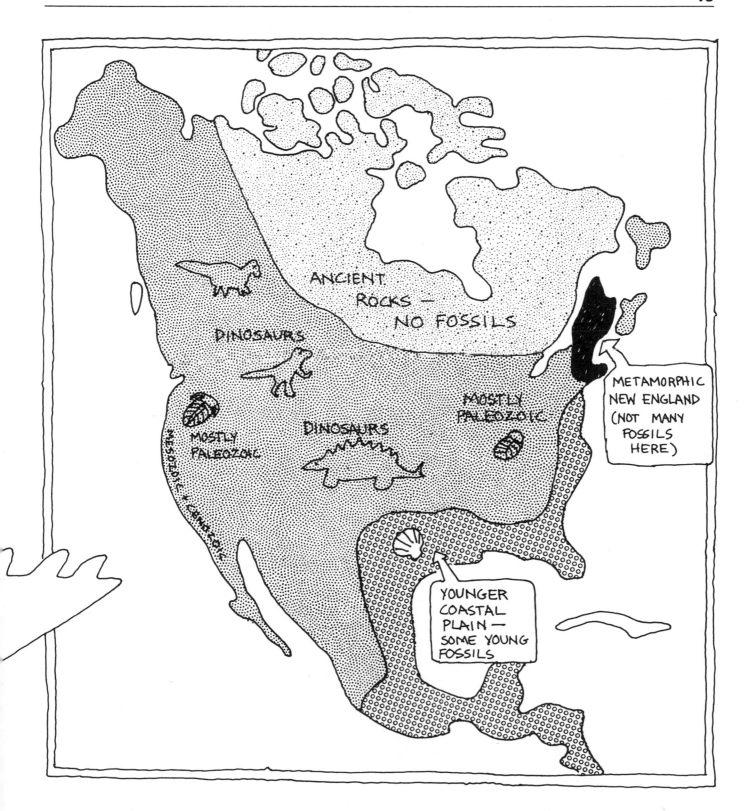

Collecting Dos and Don'ts

Use the Right Equipment

Here's what you'll need on a good fossil-hunting expedition.

1 Wear good, rough outdoor clothes, including sturdy and waterproof shoes. Always wear glasses or goggles to protect your eyes when you split open rocks.

2 A geology hammer. You need a tough hammer with either a pointed tip or a flat edge. Most paleontologists use the flat-edge style. You can buy these hammers in hardware or hobby shops.

3 Some chisels. Buy cold steel chisels, not the woodworking kind. Cheap chisels will send chips of steel flying around, so use only good-quality chisels.

4 A knapsack to carry and store everything.

5 Toilet paper to wrap your delicate fossils so that they get home safely.

6 Collecting bags of different sizes. Cloth bags, or even plastic food bags, will keep your fossils safe.

7 A small notebook to keep notes and to write labels for each fossil so that you know where you found it. It's really awful to get home and not remember where you found your fossils.

8 And it's always a good idea to bring some food and drink along. Fossil collecting is tiring work!

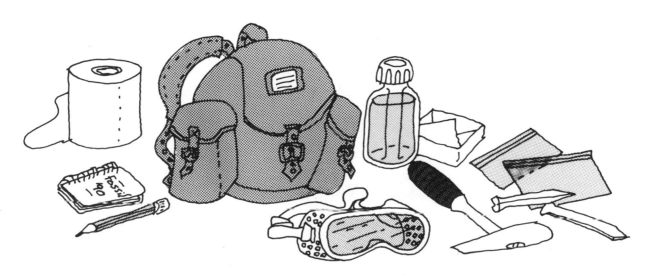

Be Careful

When collecting you must be sure to follow a few simple rules of courtesy and caution — courtesy so that you and other paleontologists will be welcomed back, and caution so that you'll stay in good shape to come back.

1 *Always go with an adult.* We don't want you to get hurt, and grown-ups have many useful purposes, such as driving the car and paying for lunch.

2 Always ask permission if you explore on private land.

3 Watch out for cars if you're collecting along a roadside, and trains if you're near railroad tracks.

4 The best fossils are often lying at the bottoms of cliffs, and you need to be extra careful in these areas. Never climb on the rocks right above someone else, and don't collect below someone climbing on a cliff. Loose rocks could easily fall and clunk the poor person underneath.

5 Snakes love to hide around and under rocks. Use your geology hammer to reach across a rock and pull it over toward you. That way the rock will always be between you and any snake. If you're collecting where there might be poisonous snakes, be sure someone in your group knows basic first aid for snakebite and where the nearest doctor's office is. *You can't be too careful.*

6 Take care when hammering. Sparks and bits of steel might fly from your hammer or chisel, so *always protect your eyes with goggles.* Also, make sure no one without goggles is standing near you when you crack rocks open!

PRIVATE PROPERTY
NO
Hunting Fishing
Swimming Spelunking
Flower Strolling
picking Eyeballing

Bumper Outcrops

Now we're all set to go on a fossil-collecting expedition. But where to go? The trick is to find an *outcrop*, where rock laid down long ago has been exposed by digging or erosion. There you won't have to dig through millions of years by yourself. In the back of this book is a list of some of the best places in America to find fossils. You can look for the one nearest you, or find a good place on your own.

One way to find an outcrop is to get in the car with an adult and just drive along, looking for rock exposures on the side of the road. Other good places are where streams and railroad tracks have cut through hills. If you live in a very flat area, visit nearby rock quarries: cement companies are always digging in limestone beds. But these places can be tricky, so always go with an adult.

When you find an outcrop, look at the kind of rock there. As you remember, fossils often come in sedimentary rock. One common type of sedimentary rock is limestone, and here's how you can tell limestone from other rocks:

1 By its color. Limestone is usually light gray, while other sedimentary rocks are dark gray, brown, or even black.

2 By the tiny grains. You usually can't see limestone grains, even with a magnifying glass.

3 By its layers. All sedimentary rocks have layers made by their grains, though limestone's grains are so tiny and so similar that sometimes it doesn't look like it has layers at all.

Bubble, Bubble, Soil and Rubble

Here's another way to identify limestone. Bring some wine vinegar from your kitchen and dribble a little on the rock. If you see tiny bubbles where the vinegar and the rock touch, then it's limestone.

Those bubbles are the signs of a chemical reaction between the acid in the vinegar and the limestone. They're full of *carbon dioxide*, the same gas we animals breathe out, and the same gas that puts the fizz in soda pop.

Fossil Spotting

You've found your outcrop, you've found your sedimentary rock, now for your fossils! Fossils really aren't hard to spot when they're around. They're usually a different color from the rock around them, and some stick out from the surface a little. Sometimes you can even recognize features, like the whorls of a snail-shell or the fronds of a fern.

The most common types of fossils are small shellfish, such as clams, snails, and ancient trilobites. Their hard shells fossilized much better than soft bodies. They've also been around a long time in the history of the earth, and they lived on the ocean floor, the best place for forming sedimentary rock which, in turn, preserves fossils.

If you see a large rock with a fossil on its outside, there might be lots of fossils inside. Make sure you're wearing your goggles, and give the rock a whack with your hammer! It will probably break right along where the fossils are. You might discover a paleontologist's treasure trove!

Digging Up More Facts

Here are some good books for amateur paleontologists to take with them or keep handy at home. They'll tell you more about how to spot fossils and help you identify the fossils you find.

Familiar Fossils of North America,
by Sidney Horenstein

The Audubon Society Field Guide to North American Fossils,
by Ida Thompson

A Field Guide to Prehistoric Life,
by David Lambert and the Diagram Group

Fossils for Amateurs: A Guide to Collecting and Preserving Invertebrate Fossils,
by Russell MacFall and Jay C. Wollin

Fossils: How to Find and Identify over 300 Genera,
by Richard Moody

Taking Care of Your Fossils

After you spot a fossil that you want to take home, chip it out of the rock with your hammer and chisels. Don't try to break the rock right next to the fossil, or you might wind up breaking the fossil as well! Instead, chip out about 1 inch (2½ cm) all around the fossil. Then wrap it up in the toilet paper, write down where you found it on a piece of paper, and put the fossil and the paper in a little bag.

You can clean the rest of the rock off your fossil when you get home. Find a clear, flat space with lots of light. Study your specimen carefully to see where your fossil ends and the rock begins. Then pick at those edges with a darning needle. Be careful you don't poke yourself.

Brush off the last bits of rock with a steel-bristled brush. Finally, wash your fossils with mild soap, and rub them dry with a soft cloth so they get a nice polish. They'll look shiny and almost new — not a day over 100 million years!

The Elusive Dinosaur

What sort of fossil are you looking for? Chances are you want to find a *Tyrannosaurus* or some other dinosaur. That's only natural, because to most people, fossils mean dinosaurs.

But think about it. If someone said, "Name a living animal," you wouldn't just think of mammals. There are lots of other animals around: birds, frogs, snakes, and fish, not to mention insects, slugs, lobsters, corals, worms — the list goes on and on.

In the same way, there were many different animals around millions of years ago, and that means many different fossils. So don't expect to stumble across a dinosaur bone right away! Keep your eye open for all kinds of fossils, from all eras of the earth's history. Fossils are fun because they tell a story, a story as fantastic as any tale about dragons or flying horses. But the tales fossils tell are true!

A Lucky Trip

Colin McEwan was a ten-year-old from Alexandria, Virginia. During a school field trip Colin climbed up a pile of dirt left by the utility company and stubbed his toe on a rock shaped like a large tin can. When he looked again that rock turned out to be a fossil — a vertebra from the spine of a plesiosaur. Now Colin's fossil find is in the Smithsonian Institution's collection, and he has a plaster cast of it for himself!

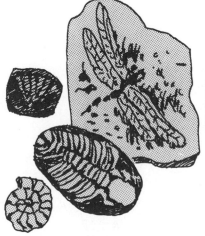

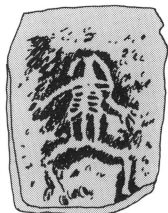

Once Upon a Time

Origins of Earth

First Fossils (bacteria)

4½ Billion

3½ Billion

YEARS AGO

So many great stories begin, "Once upon a time. . . ." But to understand what fossils have to tell us about the history of life on Earth, we first need to understand what we'll call *deep time*, time so long and vast that no one can really comprehend it.

Look at the line drawn across the top of the page. It represents the whole history of the Earth, starting with the formation of the planet 4,500 million years ago (that's 4½ *billion* years), and stretching up to this very minute. (That's looking back a long, long way.)

Now, you may think that your grandfather is old, or that the time of George Washington is way back, or the Middle Ages, or the time of the Greeks and the Romans. You could say that the Stone Age is really and truly ancient. But in deep time the Stone Age is so recent that you would need a microscope to see it on this line. Not even the time when our first human ancestors were evolving could be seen on the line, and that was over 4 million years ago!

Look where the dinosaurs fit in. Almost at the end! If dinosaurs are less than one inch from the end of the line, imagine how far back those other eight inches take us. More than nine-tenths of the history of life took place before the dinosaurs ever appeared. And more

Here, Dino!

Don't let it spoil your cartoons, but did you know that Fred Flintstone could not possibly have had a pet dinosaur? Not in a million years. In fact, not in 65 million years!

Of course there were cavemen and cavewomen, but they lived about 50 *thousand* years ago. The dinosaurs had their heyday beginning about 200 *million* years ago, then died out about 65 *million* years ago. Two hundred *million* years is a very, very long, long lonnnnng time. And a lot longer than 50 *thousand* years, which is itself a long, lonnng time. Dino and all the other dinosaurs were gone 65 million years before Fred could ever have been born!

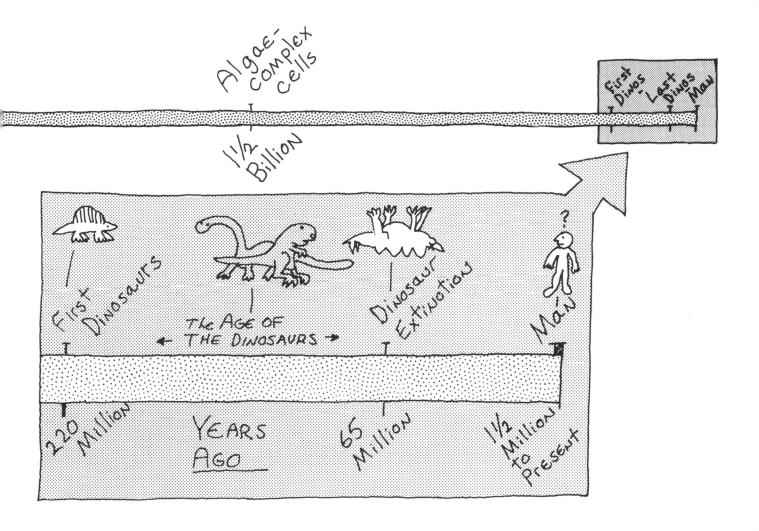

Algae-complex cells
1½ Billion

First Dinos · Last Dinos · Man

First Dinosaurs

The Age of the Dinosaurs

Dinosaur Extinction

Man

220 Million

YEARS AGO

65 Million

1½ Million to Present

than nine-tenths of all the different kinds of life that ever lived were already extinct before the first dinosaur ever shook the ground.

The Earth is very old. With this kind of time — 4,500 million years — all sorts of seemingly magical things can take place. The shape of the planet itself can change. A soup of chemicals can come to life, then change and become more complicated again and again, all the while leaving us a remarkable history written in fossils.

Right from the Start

Imagine you had an earthly time machine. Put it into warp speed and set the controls for THE BEGINNING. What would you find when you got there? No fossils, that's for sure. No life forms at all, only swirling gases and rocky meteors coming together and hardening into a great big ball — our planet Earth.

Of course, the Beginning of Earth happened about 10,000 million years after the Very Beginning of Everything. That Very Beginning is called the Big Bang. That's when all the matter in the universe exploded outward from one massive center.

The original matter from the Big Bang is the source of everything still in existence today, from fossils to chocolate fudge. Some of this matter formed the stars (including one medium-size star we call the Sun), and the stars were then drawn together into galaxies. More of the matter formed into planets circling the stars.

Luckily for us and for all the life we know, our planet, Earth, happened to be in the right place at the right time 5,000 million years ago. And lucky for us it also happened to be the right size.

If Earth had been smaller, it wouldn't have had enough gravity to hold onto the swirling collection of gases that would later become our atmosphere. If Earth had been bigger, gravity would have kept it mostly a gas planet without a surface, like Jupiter.

If Earth had been farther from the Sun, it would have been an icy planet like Pluto. Any closer and it would have been a boiling planet like Mercury. If the Sun itself had been bigger, its gravity would have swallowed us up. If the Sun had been smaller, its fire might have burned out long before now.

But just like Goldilocks' third bowl of porridge, planet Earth — 8,000 miles (13,000 km) across and 93 million miles (150 million km) from a medium-sized star — was "just

And on the outside, instead of chocolate, the Earth is covered with a *crust* made of rocks called *granite* and *basalt*.

That crust was not a pretty place 3,500 million years ago. The atmosphere was a mixture of *ammonia* (the smelly stuff in household cleaners), *hydrogen sulfide* (the smelly stuff in rotten eggs), and a deadly gas called *methane*. The only good news was that there was lots of water.

Zapped by sunlight and perhaps by lightning, some molecules of carbon and nitrogen got together with the hydrogen in the water and did something very odd. They organized themselves into tiny units that could draw in other molecules from outside and add to their strength. Later they developed ways to "reproduce" themselves completely. When that was accomplished, these chemicals had become *alive*.

In time some of these life-forms developed ways of taking energy directly from the Sun. They also began releasing oxygen into the air. The oxygen formed a protective and nurturing atmosphere around planet Earth, and from there life was really on its way. A mere 3,500 million years later, some of that very same matter from the Big Bang was organized into creatures who can read books, collect fossils, and chew bubble gum, often at the same time.

right." Not for eating, but for life to form on its surface.

Deep below the surface of the Earth there is no life, of course. When Earth was formed, gravity pulled the heaviest elements — iron and nickel — out of the gas clouds and drew them to the center, like a peanut in the middle of a piece of candy. Around that hard core formed what we call the *mantle*, a layer of hot, oozing rock 1,860 miles (3,000 km) thick — the creamy filling of that piece of candy.

Fossil Riddles (As Old as the Hills)

Try these on your friends:

1 Mount Everest is the world's tallest mountain. But what's the very tip top of Mount Everest made of? The answer is limestone — limestone *from the very bottom of the ocean floor*, containing the fossils of ancient sea life. Which is all very fine, but how the heck did the ocean floor wind up on top of a mountain?

2 Antarctica is the coldest place on earth. That's where the South Pole is, buried under miles of ice and snow even during the summer. There are no trees. All you can see is whiteness. And it's so cold that not much can live there but penguins. But guess what's sitting under all that ice and snow? Fossils of huge green tropical forests. How come?

3 The city of Chicago sits in the middle of North America, a thousand miles from the nearest ocean. Even if you've never been there, you still may have seen Chicago on the news; they show it in winter whenever they want pictures of people buried in snow! Chicago can be *very* cold. But guess what Chicago is sitting on top of. A coral reef. The kind of rock that forms tropical lagoons around islands in the South Seas. So what's the deal? A tropical sea in the cornfields outside Chicago?

The ocean floor on the top of a mountain, tropical fossils in freezing places. Something funny has been going on here. And one reason fossils are fun is that they help us to understand what our planet has been up to over the past several thousand million years. Which in turn helps us to understand even more about the history of life, a history written, partly, in fossils.

You won't have to dig in the fossil record yourself for the answers to these riddles, but you will have to dig a little deeper inside this book.

Gondwana What?

The weather changes every day, and scientists say our climate may be changing from decade to decade. But one thing we know, in part from fossils, is that our climate changed much more drastically in the past. To unravel fossil riddles, we need to understand that the earth itself used to be very, very different.

Have you ever spent time staring at the globe in your classroom: spinning it, looking at the shapes and colors, and making up games? Maybe you've imagined the islands and continents as pieces of a puzzle that could be moved around. Then your eye comes to rest on the Atlantic Ocean, with South America on one side and Africa on the other, and you think — good grief! They really do look like pieces that fit together. Maybe they were stuck together once, and later they just floated apart. Well, they could have, couldn't they?

If you ever imagined traveling continents, guess what? You were exactly right! But it was only a short while ago that scientists could accept what kids staring at the globe had been saying for years. The continents really do move, and Africa and South America and all the other continents were once part of the same giant landmass.

The earth's crust is not in one piece. It has sections called *plates*, and even though they're made of solid rock, they float across the mantle underneath. Over the years, the plates have taken the continents for quite a ride.

Dry land first emerged in chunks from underneath the ocean more than 1,000 million years ago. It was not a big deal at the time because no animals could live outside the water . . . yet.

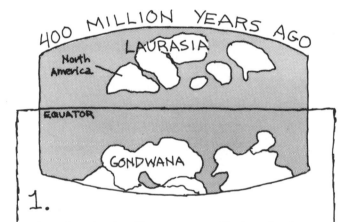

1.

Four hundred million years ago little animals were crawling out of the water onto land, but there were only two big chunks of land available. We call them *supercontinents*. Gondwana included what we now call Antarctica, Australia, Africa, South America, and India. Gondwana means "land of the Gonds," an ancient tribe from India. The other supercontinent, Laurasia, was made of most of North America, Europe, and Asia.

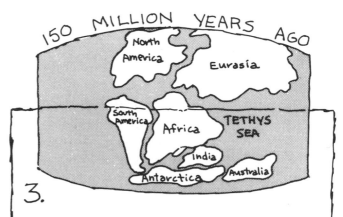

3.

Starting about 150 million years ago, a sea called Tethys created a split between Asia and Africa. North America and South America began to split away from Europe and Africa. The water between them eventually grew into the Atlantic Ocean. India, Antarctica, and Australia also began to go their separate ways to the south.

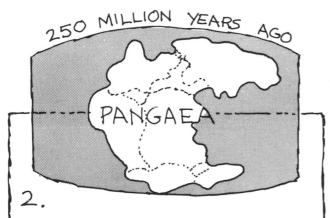

2.

Laurasia and Gondwana got together about 250 million years ago to make a super-super-continent called Pangaea. The earliest dinosaurs lived on Pangaea. They had to; there was no-where else to go. Pangaea means "all earth," and it contained all the continents on the Earth in one mass. Since all land was connected, the reptiles of this time could travel anywhere they wanted and left their fossils on every continent.

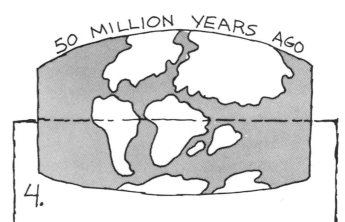

4.

A map of the earth 50 million years ago should look familiar. Central America hadn't been formed yet to connect North and South America, and Africa was still drifting on its own, but the other continents looked a lot like they do now on the globe in your classroom!

Bump and Grind

Continents are like bumper cars. They don't just float quietly. They bump and scrape or even smash right into each other!

You can see what happens in a collision between two plates by sliding two towels at each other. Their edges wrinkle up, and one towel might end up on top of the other. That's how the Himalayas, the tallest mountains in the world, got pushed up. India was moving north at full speed, and it ran smack into the rest of Asia. The bump was so hard that the Indian plate went under the Asian plate and pushed up wrinkles over 5 miles (8 km) high!

Most of the time the plates don't bump so hard. Usually they just scrape each other's edges, causing *earthquakes*. Places on the edges of plates, such as Japan and California, get lots of earthquakes, mostly small ones. But quakes can happen anywhere. One of the biggest earthquakes ever felt in North America shook Missouri in 1811.

When plates pull apart from each other, the hot mantle underneath leaks up to the surface. Right now, 5 miles (8 km) under the Atlantic Ocean, the European and North American plates are moving apart about 1 inch (2½ cm) a year. Some of the earth's mantle is pouring out of the crack and cooling into new rock on the ocean floor. There's even a volcanic island — Iceland — made of cooled down rock from deep inside the earth.

If it's hot enough, the mantle can also escape by melting a hole right through the crust. When the molten rock hits the top of the crust, it spews out as a volcano. The Hawaiian Islands were formed from mantle beneath the Pacific Ocean plate leaking through to the surface. That's why they're such "hot spots" for vacations!

Which Came First?

One hundred eighty years ago (only an instant compared to "deep time") a man named William Smith could amaze his fellow fossil collectors by looking at a fossil and telling them where it had been found. As soon as he saw one, he knew whether it came from the top of a hill, from the bottom, or in between.

William Smith wasn't a mind reader. He was a surveyor for the digging of one of England's first big canals, and that meant he did a lot of walking in the countryside. On his walks he discovered that certain kinds of fossils always appeared at the tops of hills, certain kinds at the bottoms, and certain kinds in the

Carbon Dating

Carbon dating sounds like taking a lump of coal out to a movie. Actually it's a high-tech way of figuring out just how old some fossils are.

Did you know that every living thing — even you — is a little bit radioactive? Don't worry, it's perfectly normal. The radioactivity comes from *carbon 14*, a kind of carbon atom. As we breathe and eat, we absorb carbon 14 into our bodies. If we die and fossilize, then the carbon is trapped in our fossils.

The longer an atom of carbon 14 is around, the less radioactive it becomes. That means that older fossils, with older carbon 14 in them, are less radioactive. After a fossil has been around for 50,000 years, it has no radioactivity left at all.

If paleontologists detect that a fossil has no radioactivity, they know it's more than 50,000 years old. And if it's still radioactive, they can measure how much and have a very good idea of how long ago that fossil was alive.

middle. In other words, fossils appear in layers, always in the same order.

Today William Smith wouldn't be so amazing. All paleontologists know that fossils come in layers. More important, knowing which layer a fossil comes from tells you how old it is! The oldest fossils are at the bottom, the not-so-old fossils are in the middle, and the youngest fossils are near the top. Even though those top fossils may be 500 million years old or more, the layers underneath are always older.

That's because certain kinds of plants and animals all lived at the same time, and they all left their fossils in the ground together. Then new kinds of plants and animals took over and covered the old ones. The plants and animals on the bottom became fossils, all in a layer. When the new plants and animals were replaced by even newer ones, they built another layer of fossils on top of the first, and so on right until today.

Paleontologists have given scientific names to these layers of ancient life, middle life, and recent life. But the idea of the fossils coming in layers all began with one man taking walks in the English countryside.

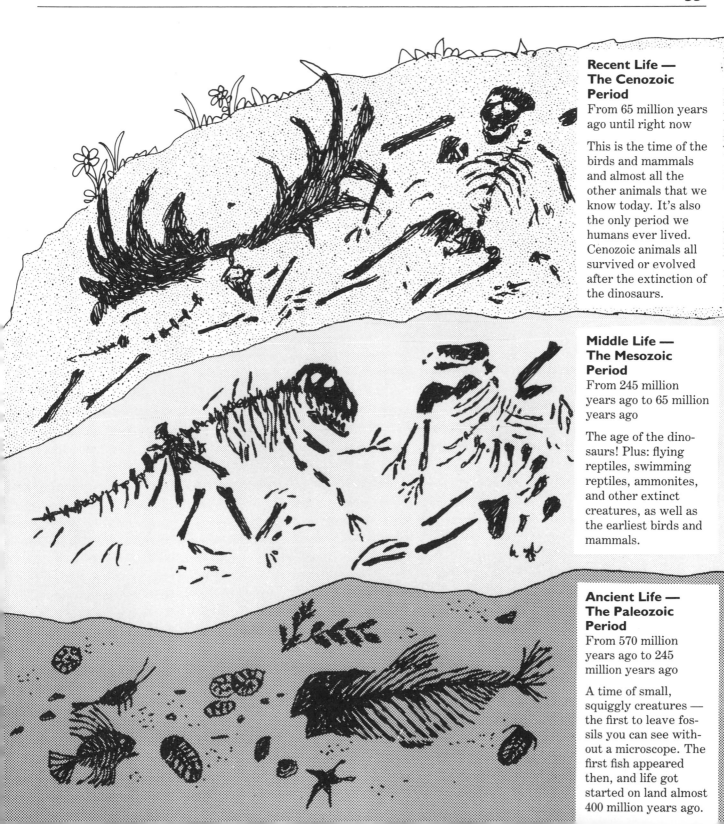

**Recent Life —
The Cenozoic
Period**

From 65 million years
ago until right now

This is the time of the
birds and mammals
and almost all the
other animals that we
know today. It's also
the only period we
humans ever lived.
Cenozoic animals all
survived or evolved
after the extinction of
the dinosaurs.

**Middle Life —
The Mesozoic
Period**

From 245 million
years ago to 65 million
years ago

The age of the dino-
saurs! Plus: flying
reptiles, swimming
reptiles, ammonites,
and other extinct
creatures, as well as
the earliest birds and
mammals.

**Ancient Life —
The Paleozoic
Period**

From 570 million
years ago to 245
million years ago

A time of small,
squiggly creatures —
the first to leave fos-
sils you can see with-
out a microscope. The
first fish appeared
then, and life got
started on land almost
400 million years ago.

A Sedimental Journey

Over millions of years, sedimentary rock can
build up in layer after layer, thousands of feet
deep. If you've ever visited the Grand Canyon
in Arizona, that's what you're looking at: layers of hardened sediments going way back in
time. Much of the earth would look the same if
we could only see it. The reason we can see
the layers in the Grand Canyon is that running
water, from the Colorado River, has cut
through the rock and exposed it like the layers
in a cake. When you drive down a highway
that has been cut through a hill of sedimentary
rock you can see the same thing, layers and
layers of sedimentary rock exposed by blasts
of dynamite.

Make Your Own Grand Canyon

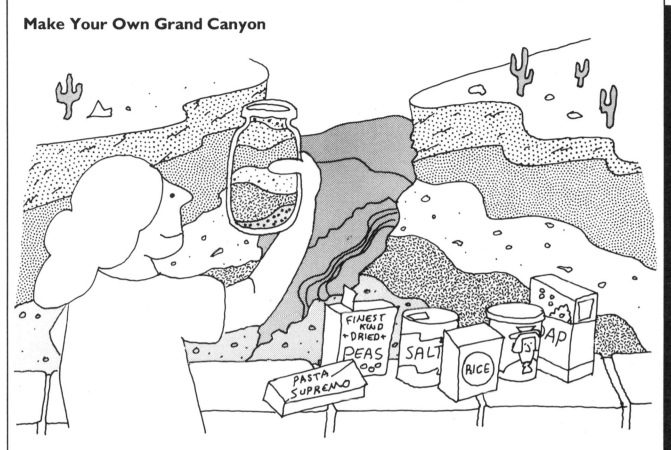

You can experiment with layering on your own. You can make a colorful sediment sculpture like the ones nature makes.

You will need
- a clear glass jar
- sugar, both brown and white
- salt, black pepper, red pepper
- kernels of unpopped popcorn
- rice
- flour
- powdered laundry detergent
- split peas
- breakfast cereal
- tiny bits of crumbled macaroni

Pour a thin layer of the sediment with the small-est grains — probably the flour — into the jar. Then pour in the sediment with the next smallest grain. Keep adding layers until you reach the top of the jar. Screw the lid on tight.

By varying the colors and thicknesses, you can make something quite beautiful. Experiment with other colorful household items, so long as everything you use stays very dry.

Nature does it differently, of course. Instead of a layer being put down all at once, each grain arrives one at a time. Then the moisture in each layer is squeezed out by the weight of the sediments above, and the grains stick together. After millions of years, you have a thick pile of rock, waiting to be carved into the Grand Canyon by rushing water.

Cool Times

A huge wall of ice and snow, 1000 feet (300 m) high, moving down from the Arctic Circle! That sounds like something out of a horror movie. But it really happened. Several times, in fact. The huge masses of snow and ice are called *glaciers*, and the times when they covered a lot of the earth are called *ice ages*.

The glaciers first spread over the land about 600 million years ago, soon after animals began to appear in the ocean. The next ice age was about 275 million years ago, before the time of the dinosaurs. The glaciers came back 2 million years ago, and they kept spreading and shrinking four times until just 10,000 years ago. Now the only glaciers you can see in North America are way up north.

Glaciers really do move. They are so heavy that the snow on top squeezes the ice on the bottom, and it starts to flow. Most glaciers slide down mountains and across valleys about 1 inch (2½ cm) a day. That's pretty slow, but steady; there's almost nothing that can stop a glacier.

Glacier ice scours down cliffs and hollows out valleys. Glaciers dug the Great Lakes this way. The walls of ice push rocks under them like bulldozers, smoothing huge stones and shoving smaller ones into huge gravel

shrink. That means there's a lot more dry land above sea level. Alaska and Siberia were connected 15,000 years ago because the ocean wasn't high enough to flow between them. The first humans arrived in North America from Asia by walking on land that's now underwater.

Here's a chilling thought: we're still living in an ice age. We're just lucky enough to live between glaciers. But there's always another coming along. Glaciers seem to come on a regular schedule, like schoolbuses. Maybe in 10,000 years North America will be under the ice again!

piles. Long Island, New York, is one such pile. In Yosemite National Park there's even a mountain, called Half Dome, that glacial ice cut right in half over thousands of years.

Glaciers, as you might expect, are very heavy. Two miles (3 km) of ice weighs a lot. New England and eastern Canada used to stick up from the Atlantic Ocean much more before a glacier sat on them. It squashed half of their land underwater! Now, with the ice melted, New England is very slowly coming up for air.

During an ice age so much of the earth's water is frozen into glaciers that the oceans

The Continental

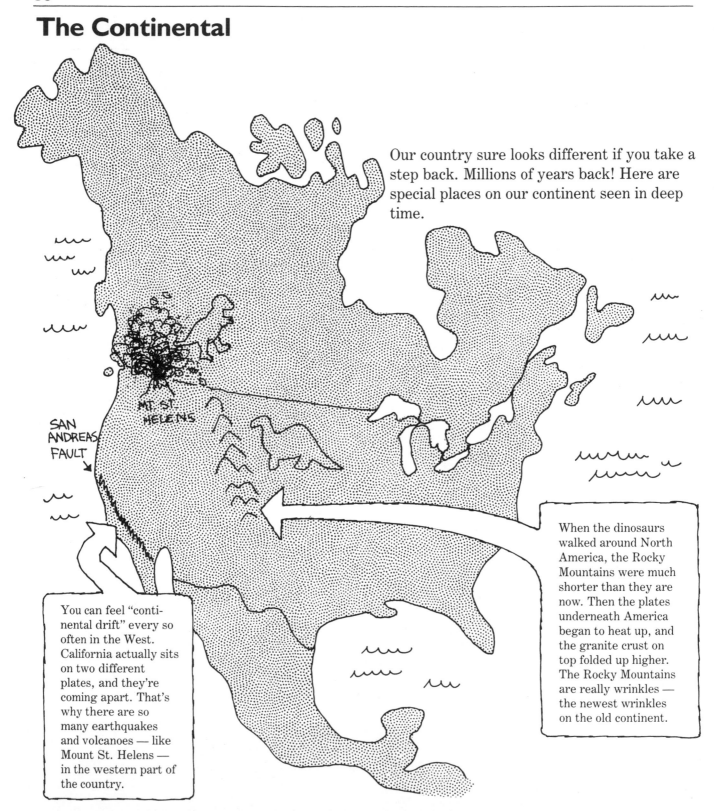

Our country sure looks different if you take a step back. Millions of years back! Here are special places on our continent seen in deep time.

MT. ST. HELENS

SAN ANDREAS FAULT

When the dinosaurs walked around North America, the Rocky Mountains were much shorter than they are now. Then the plates underneath America began to heat up, and the granite crust on top folded up higher. The Rocky Mountains are really wrinkles — the newest wrinkles on the old continent.

You can feel "continental drift" every so often in the West. California actually sits on two different plates, and they're coming apart. That's why there are so many earthquakes and volcanoes — like Mount St. Helens — in the western part of the country.

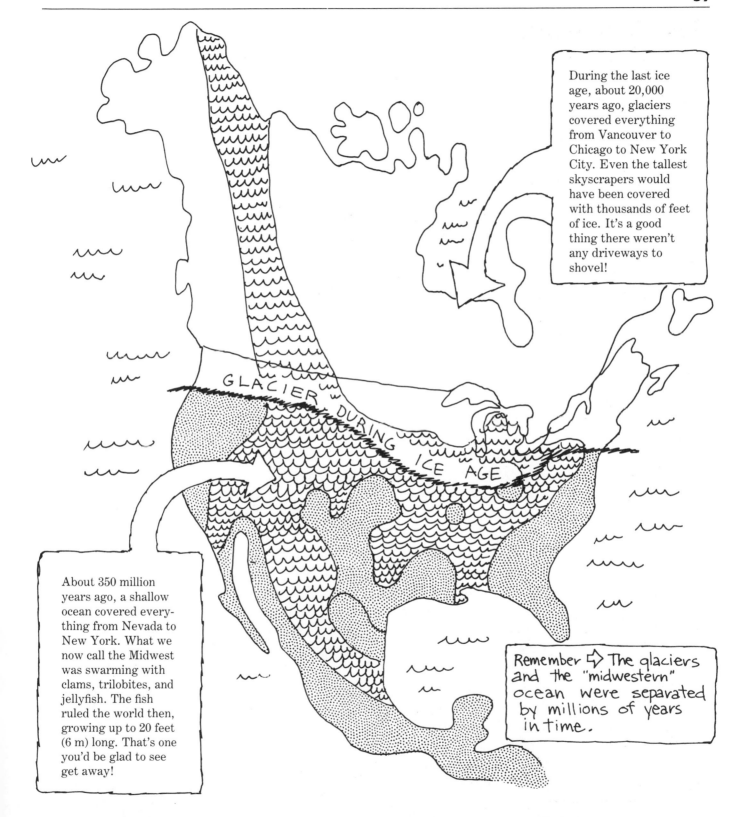

During the last ice age, about 20,000 years ago, glaciers covered everything from Vancouver to Chicago to New York City. Even the tallest skyscrapers would have been covered with thousands of feet of ice. It's a good thing there weren't any driveways to shovel!

GLACIER DURING ICE AGE

About 350 million years ago, a shallow ocean covered everything from Nevada to New York. What we now call the Midwest was swarming with clams, trilobites, and jellyfish. The fish ruled the world then, growing up to 20 feet (6 m) long. That's one you'd be glad to see get away!

Remember ⇨ The glaciers and the "midwestern" ocean were separated by millions of years in time.

Dinosaur Hunting

Professional fossil hunters know where there are hundreds of dinosaur skeletons weathering out of rocks in Utah, in Alberta, Canada, in China, and in other parts of the world. Where can *you* go to find dinosaurs?

Dinosaurs aren't as common as brachiopods. You can't just cruise out in the car and expect to pick up a dinosaur leg bone. And that's not just because dinosaur bones are heavy! They're very rare. So the best place to find a dinosaur fossil is in a museum. You'll see the bones well preserved and put together as we think they were in real life.

But what if you want to see dinosaur fossils "in the wild," the way paleontologists find them? Fortunately, in one spectacular place out west — near Vernal, Utah, to be exact — you can see dinosaur fossils sticking right out of the rock.

The United States government owns the land, and it's called Dinosaur National Monument. The government has even put up a building to protect both visitors and fossils from bad weather. One whole wall of that building is an enormous slab of rock, tilted up on its side and jam-packed with dinosaur bones — *Allosaurus*, *Apatosaurus* (the real name of *Brontosaurus*), and other giants.

These dinosaurs belong to everyone, since they're on government land. Besides,

they're too big to carry home. Here anyone can see dinosaur fossils unassembled, in the same sandstone they've been lying in for over 150 million years!

In the eastern United States you can see scads of dinosaur footprints left in the ground at Dinosaur State Park, near the town of Rocky Hill, Connecticut. Over 200 million years ago dinosaurs walked back and forth over the gooey mud on the shore of an ancient lake. The footprints they left got filled with other muds, preserving them for us today. You can even make casts of the footprints to take home with you.

Three-toed dinosaur prints look like giant versions of bird footprints. The first person to study them, back in the early 1800s, thought they actually were prints from enormous birds! No one had heard of dinosaurs then. Now paleontologists are pretty sure that birds are basically feathered dinosaurs, so that old paleontologist's guess doesn't look so bad, does it?

In the back of this book we've listed many good dinosaur museums and national parks where you can see fossils. But remember, don't take anything away! Fossils in those places are meant to be shared with all visitors.

Living Fossils

Living fossils aren't dinosaur skeletons that have come to life. They're animals that have been on earth for millions of years without changing. These creatures were so well adapted that they never became extinct or evolved any further. Finding them is another way of exploring the fossil record.

For instance, whenever you see a horseshoe crab scuttling through the shallow water near the beach — and you can see them anywhere along the Atlantic coast from Nova Scotia to Mexico — it's like looking at a time traveler from 250 million years ago! That's how long these little guys have been around, almost unchanged. The dinosaurs have come and gone, as have the saber-toothed tigers and cave-dwelling humans, yet the horseshoe crabs have kept right on going about their lives in pretty much the same old way as if nothing were different.

And the cockroaches that everyone hates? Creatures very like them were hiding in the shadows when *Tyrannosaurus* went thundering by. No wonder they're so hard to get rid of!

Here are some living fossils and how long they've been around. Look at the time line at the end of the book to get an idea of how much of life has changed while these creatures have stayed almost the same, and just who those cockroaches may have been rubbing elbows with way back when.

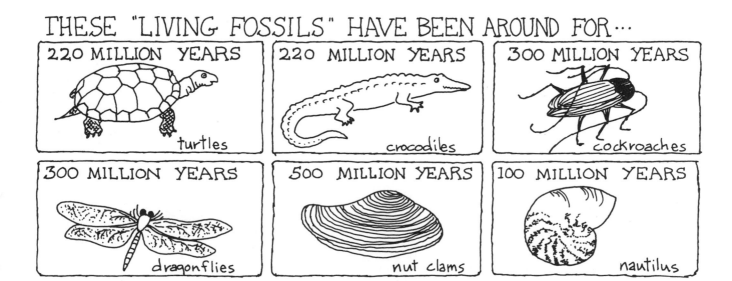

THESE "LIVING FOSSILS" HAVE BEEN AROUND FOR···

220 MILLION YEARS — turtles

220 MILLION YEARS — crocodiles

300 MILLION YEARS — cockroaches

300 MILLION YEARS — dragonflies

500 MILLION YEARS — nut clams

100 MILLION YEARS — nautilus

Double Treat on the Beach

Beachcombing is a lot like fossil collecting. Take off your shoes and amble along the *strand line*, that snaky pile of junk that runs along the upper part of the beach, marking the highest point of the high tide. Poke around and you'll find lots of goodies — sand fleas, of course, but lots of other creatures cast up from beneath the ocean.

Clams and snail shells will probably head the list. But also jumbled up in the seaweed there will be strings of snail and fish eggs, sponge pieces, maybe some coral (along southern beaches), and our own personal favorite, horseshoe crab skeletons.

When you think about it, these modern-day beach treasures are a lot like fossils. Someday, millions of years from now, paleontologists would think they've hit a fossil gold mine if they could find just a fraction of the shells we can go out and pick up off the beach whenever we want.

Or look at it the other way around: suppose you had a time machine and could go back 380 million years to a beach when life was just moving onto land. That's very much like what you're doing when you drive to a roadside outcrop in central New York, hop out of the car, and start picking up brachiopod and coral fossils.

The moral of the story is that any trip to a beach is a trip in a fossil time machine, with the time set to RIGHT NOW. And those shells and pieces of sponge and coral are just as neat as an ancient snail or ammonite.

But there's more to the beach than modern fossils-in-the-making. In some places, like along the Pacific Ocean south of San Francisco, you can find real fossils sticking out of the rocks overlooking the beach! In Maryland, along the shores of Chesapeake Bay, the cliffs are made of soft sand, so many of the fossils have tumbled down onto the beach, and they look confusingly like modern seashells.

If you're not sure whether something is a fossil or a modern shell, here are a couple of clues. Fossils are usually heavier than shells. Most fossils are all one color, usually dark gray or white. Seashells are often colored with pretty designs, which is why many people collect them.

Caught in the Act

Ever hop on some rocks along a beach and stumble on a *tide pool*, a puddle of water left stranded as the tide pulled out? Take a look at this little community of living things next time you're near a rocky beach. There's no need to collect the little snails, sea anemones, sea urchins, and crustaceans living in there. Just watch them as they wave their tentacles (anemones feed and take in oxygen this way), or scuttle around (crabs love tide pools), or slowly and slimily creep their way around (snails glide along on a mucus-covered foot, which sounds disgusting but does the job very nicely).

Collect with your eyes; the shells on the beach are dead remains, but the creatures in the tide pool still deserve their day under the sun. This is a good, easy way to get a feel for how sea creatures have lived for the last 600 million years. Look at the tide pool animals and plants and think of them when you're out collecting dried-up fossils millions of years old!

What, No Fossils Near You?

Maybe the next time you're traveling on vacation you can get your parents to include a side trip to one of the fossil hot spots listed in the back of this book.

But what if you can't wait for a vacation trip? There's still a trick that may get you near plenty of fossils right in your own town, no matter where you live. There's a catch, though. These fossils you can't take home. You can see them, even touch them. But you can't bash them out of the rock — because they're in places like lamps, coffee tables, the stairs in your school, and the sidewalks in your town.

They could be in the walls of any office building downtown in any city. They might be in the counter of your bank or in the bathrooms of just about any older public building in any city or town. Museums, libraries, town halls, and schools are all great places to explore for fossils.

Why are fossils sticking out of so many floors and walls all over the place? Rocks are often cut out of the ground to be used as building stones. Some of the rock is granite, with no fossils. But limestone is also very popular as a building stone, and it is often crammed full of fossils. When the builders smooth out the rocks and polish them, they cut through some fossils and reveal them in beautiful shining profile. One popular, light-colored limestone from Texas is just full of clam fossils!

So how do you make a "collection" of building-stone fossils? You do it with your *mind*. Make a game out of it. Keep a list of all the unusual fossils you've spotted. Find out how many different places in your area have fossils sticking out of the walls. See which of your group of friends can build the longest list of finds, and try to figure out what sorts of fossils you find. (Here's a hint: brachiopods, corals, snails, and sea lily stems are the most common.)

Remember: you don't always have to hold the specimen in your hand for it to belong to your "collection." Many big game hunters traded their rifles in for cameras long ago; now they collect their "trophies" on film. A lot of the thrill of fossil collecting is simply in the discovery!

Assembly Required

Fossils don't come "fully assembled." They don't even come with directions. The fossils that you find in rocks never look like those awesome dinosaur skeletons or life-size models you see standing in museums. Those were put together by many paleontologists working for a long time.

When you find a fossil skeleton in the ground, it looks more like a big jumbled mess. After the animal died, its body could have been chewed on by other animals or washed by a stream into a big mixed-up pile. Often some bones are missing.

If you find a shellfish fossil, like a snail, you're lucky. Snailshells come in only one piece. But putting a fossil skeleton together is like doing a jigsaw puzzle in three dimensions.

And the worst part is that even when you have all the bones, you don't have all the pieces of the puzzle. You don't have the skin or muscles or the ligaments that held the skeleton together. You don't have the animal's eyes or ears, fur, feathers, or claws. Those are some of the most interesting parts of the body, but they're too soft to petrify, so we almost never find them.

For the detective who pieces the clues together, some solutions make sense and others don't. The more we know about basic biology — how creatures live and compete and reproduce — the better we'll be at making sense of what fossils try to tell us.

In the Living World

Paleontologists have a thing about fossils, naturally. But fossils are dead. *Very* dead. No self-respecting fossil is less than 10,000 years old, and most are much older than that — millions and millions of years old, usually. But paleontologists don't like only dead animals and plants. We need to know about living ones just as much, so we can do better at figuring out how ancient creatures lived.

Part of the trick is knowing how individual creatures operate. The rest is knowing how plants and animals operate together within their neighborhoods. You can guess all you want that a certain ancient beast had a certain kind of tooth to crack open acorns, but it's not a very good guess if you can't prove there were oak trees around to produce those acorns!

You can study and "collect" animals and plants in your own neighborhood, and get to know some of the many different kinds of insects, mammals, birds, trees, and other plants. This is just like making a fossil collection, only these items are still alive.

Of course, you really don't want to collect things like birds and mammals. In most places, animals are protected by law. They deserve our protection so we don't drive them the way of the dinosaurs and so many other kinds of ancient life: to extinction.

Yet you can collect just by using your eyes. Take a walk in the nearest field or woodlot. Can you identify five different kinds of trees? Can you tell evergreens, such as long-needled pines, from hardwoods, like maples? Do you know the difference between a maple and an oak? (Hint: compare the shapes of their leaves, and the kinds of seeds or nuts they make.)

How about the birds in your neighborhood? It's good practice for fossil collecting to know how to tell the different species of living animals apart before you try to do the same thing with fossils. Do you know robins? Crows? Woodpeckers?

Have a contest with your friends. Who can make the longest list of different species of birds, mammals, and plants in your neighborhood?

Skin and Bones

A pink polka dot *Allosaurus* sounds like something out of a bad dream, but what if *Allosaurus* really was pink and spotted?

Since nobody ever saw dinosaurs "in the flesh," nobody knows what color their flesh was. Most fossils tell us only about bones, the dinosaurs' insides. We have to guess what their outsides looked like.

Paleontologists guess about dinosaur colors based on the colors of their modern relatives. The dinosaurs' nearest reptile relatives are crocodiles, and because crocs are green, most people think dinosaurs were green, too. But some paleontologists say that the dinosaurs' nearest living relatives are birds, and birds come in every color of the rainbow!

There are two reasons why dinosaurs may have evolved with brightly colored skin. The first was for camouflage. Spotted dinosaurs would be able to hide in the jungle, the way jaguars and giraffes do. Or they might have used colors to attract the opposite sex. As a peacock unfolds his tail for a peahen, a proud dinosaur could have shown off its bright colors to its mate.

So you can imagine dinosaurs in almost any color you want, and no one can prove you wrong. How about a red-breasted *Brachiosaurus?* Or a *Stegosaurus* with stripes?

Dinosaur Detectives

To find out what the animals who left fossils really looked like, paleontologists have to be detectives. They search for clues and evidence, such as:

1 Where did the fossil come from? You shouldn't find clams living in a forest, or woolly mammoths on the bottom of the ocean.

2 What other fossils were nearby? Those other fossils could come from what your animal ate, or what ate it.

3 Does the fossil look like any animals alive today? Animals that are closely related, or animals that behave the same, usually have similar bodies.

Like a police artist sketching a suspect from a description, paleontologists put together a picture of what a dinosaur looked like from all the fossil clues they know. As they get more clues, that picture might change. Our ideas about dinosaurs have changed a lot as paleontologists discovered more information.

For instance, you've probably seen pictures of *Stegosaurus*, but did you ever see two different pictures like these? *Stegosaurus*'s fossil bones were found a century ago, and ever since then paleontologists have been trying to make up their minds about what *Stegosaurus* really looked like.

It had plates of armor sticking up from its back, but did they come in twos, or one at a time? How long was that tail, and did it really have spikes sticking out of it? The back legs of *Stegosaurus* are twice as tall as the front legs, so how fast could it walk?

The picture on the right is the latest picture of what *Stegosaurus* looked like. There is one row of plates, slanting left and right. Its tail stuck out, instead of dragging along the ground, and it had four spikes on the end. *Stegosaurus* could probably walk pretty fast, and maybe even rear up on its hind legs. Which picture do you like better, the new *Stegosaurus* or the old?

Iggy Pop

Iguanodon was a large, plant-eating dinosaur that left some very important — and puzzling — fossils. It lived only in swamps, but in the warm climate of 120 million years ago there were swamps all over the world. Paleontologists have found *Iguanodon* fossils in North America, South America, Europe, Asia, Africa, and even on an island that's now north of the Arctic Circle.

Iguanodon had a sharp beak and teeth like an iguana (*Iguanodon* means "iguana tooth"), so it must have chewed on leaves and twigs like that modern lizard. But it was much larger than any lizard: 30 feet (9 m) long, and 5 tons (4½ MT) heavy.

Because *Iguanodon* lived in so many different parts of the world it was one of the first dinosaur fossils to be discovered. In 1822 an Englishwoman named Mary Ann Mantell spotted some fossilized *Iguanodon* teeth in a pile of rock while she was taking a walk. She brought them home and examined them with her husband, Gideon. Later they published a book about their discovery. Gideon did the writing and Mary Ann drew the pictures. The Mantells were two of the first dinosaur paleontologists.

One of the biggest mysteries to solve about *Iguanodon* is its spiky thumb. Paleontologists aren't sure what it was used for: fighting or grabbing onto things. For a while they even thought the spike belonged on the tip of the *Iguanodon* nose, like a rhinoceros horn!

Stuck on Fossils

Here's a really sticky fossil problem to solve. Paleontologists found lots of fossils from the last ice age at one site in California. That's the La Brea Tar Pits, where gooey tar deposits appeared about 14,000 years ago. In fact, *brea* means "tar" in Spanish.

Animals who wandered over the tar got stuck and never got out. They sank down into the gluey goop and died. Their skeletons became fossils. Now it's our job to figure out from those fossils what the Ice Age was really like.

There are more fossils from meat-eating animals in the La Brea Tar Pits than from plant-eating animals. For instance, paleontologists counted about 600 *Parapavo* fossils. They were birds, much like turkeys, who walked on the ground — and into the tar. But the tar also caught almost 1,000 golden eagles, high-flying birds of prey. And while 130 horses wandered into the tar, there were over 1,600 Dire Wolves!

Does that mean that 14,000 years ago, there were lots more carnivores than herbivores? That doesn't make sense, judging from what we can see today in Africa. Huge herds of antelopes, zebras, and gazelles eat grass, and only a few lions, cheetahs, and leopards eat the antelopes, zebras, and gazelles. If there were too many more meat-eaters, there wouldn't be enough meat to go around.

So how can we explain the mystery of the fossils in the La Brea Tar Pits? Try imagining that you're a plant-eating animal in the Ice Age. What would you do if you got stuck in a tar pit? You'd yell for help. LOUD!

Now imagine that you're a meat-eater in the Ice Age, and you hear a helpless herbivore yelling. What would you do? You'd run to find yourself some free food — and you'd get stuck in the tar pit, too! (Nobody ever said meat-eaters in the Ice Age were all that smart.)

That's why there are more fossils of meat-eating animals in the La Brea Tar Pits, even though there have always been more plant-eating animals around. For every plant-eater that got stuck in the tar, a whole bunch of meat-eaters went rushing in after it.

You can still visit the La Brea Tar Pits on Wilshire Boulevard in Los Angeles. Many of the fossils that were found there are on display in a museum next door.

The World's Biggest Model Airplane

"Could *Quetzalcoatlus* fly?" paleontologists asked. *Quetzalcoatlus* was a huge pterodactyl with a big head and no tail. That's not a very good shape for flying, and paleontologists worried that it couldn't get off the ground. Some thought that *Quetzalcoatlus* just glided down from cliffs and tall trees, and then had to climb back up again for another glide.

Paleontologists can't go out and watch *Quetzalcoatlus* take off; it's been extinct for over 70 million years. So some scientists built their own *Quetzalcoatlus*. They followed the design of the fossil skeleton and built a model 20 feet (6 m) across. They used electric motors to power the wings and a computer to tell it where to go.

The model builders launched their *Quetzalcoatlus* from a sort of motorized slingshot out in the Arizona desert, and it flew! It flapped its wings, flew in circles, and stayed in the air for five minutes — long enough for a *Quetzalcoatlus* to catch its food. Then the scientists took the model to Washington, D.C., for a public demonstration. And it crashed.

So what's the answer to the mystery of whether *Quetzalcoatlus* could fly? Evolutionary, my dear Watson. It probably could, but it wasn't easy.

The First Fossils

Life has gotten a lot more complicated since the oldest fossils were laid down, about 3,500 million years ago. The creatures that left them were very simple, like the bacteria around today. Their fossils can be seen only with microscopes. For 2,000 million years all of life was bacteria, creatures made of just one cell. Today you have billions of cells in your own body!

That growth came about through *evolution*. Evolution means change. It explains how we humans emerged from this long chain of life.

Kids look a little like their mothers and a little like their fathers. That's because each baby receives a tiny packet of instructions from each parent when the baby first starts to grow as a single cell in its mother's womb. The single cell divides into more cells, which specialize and become skin or muscle or bone. The information — whether to be short or tall, to have brown eyes or blue — is carried within each cell in chemical bundles called *genes*.

Different genes make each creature different, and as a result some creatures survive better than others. Fast rabbits can run away from foxes. Tall daisies can catch the sun. Smart sea gulls can figure out how to open up a clam shell to get to the meat. Slow rabbits, short daisies, and dumb sea gulls have a much harder time surviving.

It makes sense that a fast rabbit that can outrun foxes will live a little longer than the others. A fast rabbit that lives longer also has more time to have babies. So the next generation of bunnies, the ones that inherit the "fast" genes from their fast parents, will also live longer and have more babies. After a while the fast bunnies have taken over, and the slow bunnies have died out. This is the process called *natural selection*, first described by an Englishman named Charles Darwin in 1859.

Climbing Our Family Tree

BACTERIA

Family trees are charts showing parents and children, grandparents and great-grandchildren, back to your earliest ancestors. They show how people are related to each other, and how the family genes came down to you. You might have a family tree that goes back to the time of the Revolutionary War or further, but did you know that our human family tree goes back to the first fossils?

Our earliest ancestor is the same as every other living creature's earliest ancestor. Every plant and animal on earth is descended from the same simple bacteria, which means that we're all relatives! The same basic genetic material in one-celled creatures is also found in you. Even plants, some of our most distant relatives, have the same cell structure as we do.

The more we resemble other animals, the closer we're related to them. Humans and chimpanzees look a lot alike, and in fact we're pretty close relatives: we had the same ancestor alive only five million years ago. Humans and birds don't look so much alike because we've been evolving separately since late in the Paleozoic era 250 million years ago. (*Paleozoic* was explained back in the "Which Came First?" chapter.) And we don't look anything like worms (hooray!), which are some of our most distant animal relatives. We're still related to them, though.

We're even related to the dinosaurs! We're not direct descendants, of course, but we and the dinosaurs had the same reptile ancestors 300 million years ago. So the next time you meet a *Megalosaurus* walking down the street, say, "Howdy, cousin!"

Pure Shellfishness

Long before there were dinosaurs — in fact, before there were any animals on land — *invertebrates* (animals without backbones) swam around in the ancient seas. From 575 million years to 400 million years ago marine invertebrates were the biggest, most advanced creatures alive — the rulers of the prehistoric earth!

Marine invertebrates came in all shapes and sizes. Looking at their fossils shows how many ways the first life evolved. They're the earliest animals we could see on our family tree. You might recognize them while you're out fossil hunting, at the beach, or even at your dinner table!

Slow and Steady

We know more about ancient *snails* than about jellyfish because of their coiled shells. Hard snail shells make much better fossils than soft jellyfish bodies, as well as giving animals protection, strength, and a home of their own. But shells also create some problems, like having to carry a whole house everywhere!

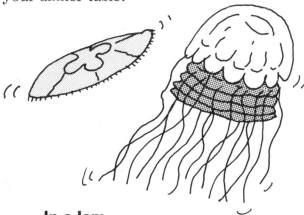

In a Jam

Jellyfish might have been among the first animals you could have seen without a microscope, 600 million years ago. But we can't be sure, because their bodies are so soft (they're not called "jellyfish" for nothing) that they usually don't fossilize. You can see them today on both coasts of North America.

Two of a Kind

Clams and *brachiopods* are both shellfish with two hinged shells. How can you tell them apart? Brachiopods use muscle power to open their shells, so when their muscles stop working, their shells stay closed. Clams are just the opposite. They use their muscles to close their shells. When they relax or die, their shells automatically pop open. If you find the two fossil shells stuck together, chances are it was a brachiopod. If the shells are apart, you've got a clam.

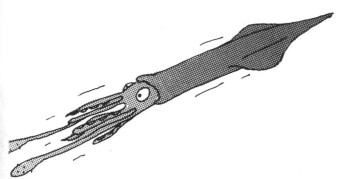

The Jet Set

Squids, octopuses, and *ammonites* were all jet propelled long before jet engines were invented! These invertebrates took water into a sac in the front of their body, then squirted it out through a spout, and the force of the squirt pushed them along. Squids, octopuses, and the beautiful pearly nautilus still zip around by jet propulsion today.

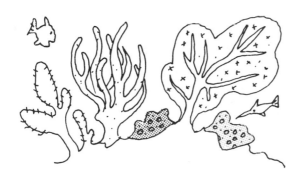

Going Nowhere

On the other hand, *corals* and *crinoids* didn't move at all. These invertebrates looked a lot like plants — crinoids are also called "sea lilies" — but they breathed oxygen like all other animals. They ate by filtering little bits of food from the seawater that flowed through their bodies. Corals sometimes lived right on top of each other, building up long reefs where hundreds of different fish swam.

A Squirt of a Squid

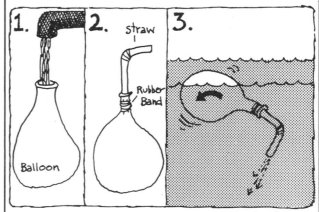

You can watch how squids move through the water in your own bathtub, and you don't even need a squid. (Good thing, too; some squid are 20 feet (6 m) long!)

You will need
- a balloon
- a drinking straw that bends in the middle
- a rubber band
- a bathtub full of water.

1 Fill the balloon with water.

2 Put the straw into the spout of the balloon and snap the rubber band around the spout to seal it tight.

3 Drop the balloon into the bathtub and watch it take off! The stretched-out walls of the balloon will bounce back and push the water out in a jet, and the jet will push the balloon across the tub.

4 Try some steering. Leave the straw straight and the balloon will move in a straight line. Point the straw back at the balloon and the balloon will move in the opposite direction. Bend the straw out to one side and the balloon will spin around in a circle. Squids have the same sort of spout to control where they go.

Trilobites

ISOTELUS

One special group of ancient shellfish that left lots and lots of fossils are the trilobites. You can recognize them by the three lengthwise sections on their bodies (*trilobite* means "divided into three lobes, or bulging parts").

Trilobites had hard outer skeletons, like suits of armor, which they had to shed to grow. Each growing trilobite would leave behind many shells — all the more reason why so many fossil trilobites have been found. To understand what trilobites really looked like, we paleontologists have to remember to add a pair of antennae and many legs, which hardly ever fossilized.

Even though their shells were hard, trilobites could bend and move because their bodies were divided into many segments. The more ridges along their back, the more flexible they were. Some trilobites could even bend their backs all the way around.

You can see how that works by looking at "pill bugs" or "curly-bugs," which scientists call *isopods*. These little creatures, about ½

inch (1 cm) long, might be living in your garden. They are crustaceans with hard shells, like lobsters and crabs, but their backs come in many segments. When they're in trouble they roll into a tight little ball to protect themselves. Watching pill bugs walk around your garden is almost like watching trilobites scuttle around on the ancient seafloor.

Trilobites came in many strange forms. *Phacops* could look forward, backward, and sideways at the same time because both of its bulging eyes had many lenses. *Deltacephalaspis* had long spikes on either side of its head, and *Greenops* had a spiky, star-shaped tail. *Isotelus* ranged in size from little babies to 2-foot-long (60 cm) monsters.

Isotelus used to live in Ohio, but you won't see any trilobites alive in Cleveland anymore. About 250 million years ago, at the end of the Paleozoic era, all the trilobites went extinct.

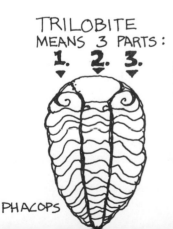

TRILOBITE MEANS 3 PARTS:
1. 2. 3.

PHACOPS

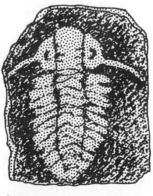

DELTACEPHALASPIS FOSSIL

Ex-animals

When does an animal go extinct? When every single animal in a species has died and no babies are left behind. Because each species is unique, we'll never see that animal again — only its fossils, if we're lucky.

Over 200,000 years ago the Irish elk wandered all over Ireland, England, and Europe, which were connected during the Ice Age. It didn't hunt anybody and was probably pretty gentle. The Irish elk was taller than a moose, and its antlers could grow as big as 11 feet (3½ m) across. Those horns were probably the most beautiful thing about the Irish elk, but we'll never know because the species has been extinct for 10,000 years.

Irish elks were hunted by lions and wolf packs, and sometimes they got stuck in the Irish peat bogs. But those aren't the reasons they went extinct. Irish elks were adapted to those troubles. There were always more mating pairs to have babies and carry on the species. But about 10,000 years ago they started dying off faster than they could reproduce. Eventually there was only one Irish elk left, and then none, and we don't know why.

When many different species of plants and animals all die out at about the same time, that's called a *mass extinction*. It means that something terrible damaged the whole environment. Mass extinctions are the biggest mysteries that paleontologists have to solve. It's like figuring out thousands of murder mysteries all at once. Unfortunately, mass extinctions leave only a few surviving species and fossils to tell the tale.

Danger!

Endangered species are animals and plants that might go extinct very quickly because of what we humans are doing today. They won't die out over thousands of years, like the trilobites, but could be gone in as little as ten years. Many animals just can't adapt quickly enough to changes created by humans.

There were millions of passenger pigeons alive in George Washington's time. When their flocks flew south for the winter, they could block out the sun for hours. But people killed them off by cutting down the forest habitat where they lived and by hunting them for sport. The last passenger pigeon died in the Cincinnati Zoo in 1914, and we'll never see another. Passenger pigeons vanished in less than a century after surviving for more than 15,000 years.

It's Easy Being Green

What can you make out of fresh air, water, and sunshine? Besides a great day at the beach, you might think, "not much." But those few elements are all a plant needs to live. From sunshine, water, and the carbon dioxide in air, plants make sugar — their food — and oxygen — which we animals breathe. That's called *photosynthesis*, or "building from light." They use a chemical in their cells called *chlorophyll*, which is also what makes plants green.

The first plants were one-celled algae, and they're still the most common living creatures in the world. Algae have been living in the ocean for over 3,500 million years, and you can see them floating in water and hanging off piers today. Algae provide most of the oxygen we breathe, but they're very simple plants. Each one is microscopically small, and they can't live outside the water.

By 380 million years ago, moss plants were spreading over the land. Simple algae is an ancestor of moss but moss's cells are more complicated. There are different kinds of cells for sucking up water, for making sugar, and for reproducing. Even so, moss is tiny and very primitive. The thick green patches you see on walls and trees are actually thousands of tiny moss plants bunched together.

Moss plants were living on land 380 million years ago, but they weren't living on dry land. They had to stick to moist places to get their water. Then new plants evolved to store

water in their stems. That's a big change, like keeping a glass of water next to your bed instead of having to go into the bathroom in the middle of the night!

The first plants with real stems, roots, and leaves were club mosses and horsetails. Then came the ferns. They're all still around, but not like they used to be. The tallest they grow now is about 3 feet (1 m). But 350 million years ago, when there weren't any other kinds of plants around, some were as tall as trees!

Who lived in the swampy forests made of club mosses, horsetails, and ferns? Insects, the same animals who live on those plants today. But 350 million years ago insects were huge. Some dragonflies measured 2½ feet (75 cm) from wingtip to wingtip. A few centipedes were 20 feet (6 m) long. And cockroaches were already walking around wherever they wanted, just as they do today.

Club mosses, horsetails, and ferns reproduce with spores instead of seeds. If you look on the bottom of fern leaves, you can see brown spots about the size of a pencil eraser. Each of those is a spore-sac, jammed full of tiny reproductive cells.

Green Slime

Here's a way to watch how primitive fungus spread all over the world — like slime.

You will need
- a clear glass jar with a lid
- a slice of bread
- water

1 Put a slice of bread in the glass jar.

2 Poke three tiny holes in the lid of the jar.

3 Add a few drops of water to the bread and screw the lid on.

4 Look at the slice of bread through the jar every day. Soon you'll see dots of bluish-green fuzz start to grow on the bread. If you wait a few days more, the fuzz will grow into big clumps. Don't open the jar, or you'll let the fuzz get all over your house!

5 When you finish watching the fuzz grow, throw the jar away — carefully.

That blue-green fuzz is bread mold. It comes in tiny spores, just like algae, moss, and baby ferns. Mold spores are floating in the air all around us. You trap some in the jar when you seal it. All they need to grow is a little bread for food and some water. The spots you see are thousands of mold spores crowded together. With enough air, water, and bread, they can keep multiplying forever.

Something Fishy

There's a new kind of fossil in rocks about 500 million years old. That means that a new group of animals appeared on the earth then: the *vertebrates*. Instead of living in shells, vertebrates have hard bones, such as a backbone, inside their bodies. Having a skeleton made it a lot easier for them to grow and to move around, even though not having armor meant more cuts and scrapes.

The first vertebrates were fish, which still had stiff bony armor as well as backbones. They didn't even have jaws. Instead they had little holes for mouths, and they had to suck in their food — algae, plankton, and other tiny things. Lampreys still don't have jaws today. They live by attaching themselves to fish with their mouths and sucking out blood. They're fish vampires!

Maybe you've heard that fish breathe water, but really they breathe oxygen, just like we do. The difference is that they have to get their oxygen through the water. Luckily, most water has oxygen molecules dissolved in it. As a fish's gills move, they filter the oxygen molecules out of the water and into the fish's body. In some ponds you won't find any fish at all because pollution has removed all the oxygen from the water. The fish had nothing to breathe, and they all suffocated.

By 350 million years ago fish had evolved into the largest and strongest animals around, and the largest and strongest of the fish was *Dinichthys*, a terror of the seas! It had thick armor all over its head and shoulders, but nowhere else. (Paleontologists have to guess at the rest of its shape.) What look like teeth were actually spiky parts of *Dinichthys*'s head armor. In Ohio paleontologists found fossils from a *Dinichthys* that must have been over 20 feet (6 m) long. It was the first Jaws!

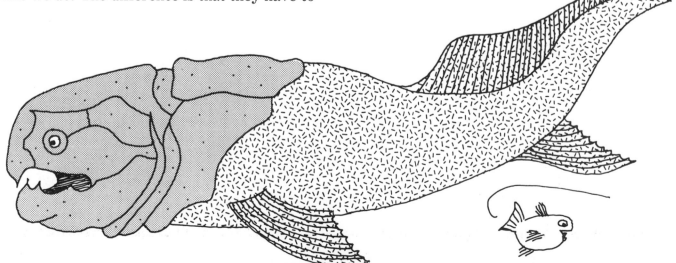

Amphibious Landings

Everybody out of the water!

Some fish didn't have any choice. The pools where they lived were getting too shallow, so they had to crawl out onto the land.

Some early fish already had lungs, as well as gills, to breathe air. Some could push themselves along the ground with their bony fins. Once they were on land, they discovered there was lots to eat; plants had been growing out of the water for millions of years, and many insects and spiders had already arrived. The early fish who stayed on land became the amphibians.

Amphibian means "creature that lives in both places." Amphibians are born and grow up in water, but they move to land as adults. They go back into the water only to find food and to lay their eggs. Frogs, toads, salamanders, and caecilians (which look like worms) are all the modern amphibians. But 280 million years ago they had big cousins like *Eryops*, 6 feet (2 m) long and 200 pounds (90 kg). If you touched *Eryops* you wouldn't have gotten warts, but you might have gotten your hand chomped: *Eryops* was a meat-eater!

If you've ever touched a frog you know that its back feels slimy. That's mucus, and it stops the frog's skin from drying out. Amphibians have to keep their skin wet so that they can absorb extra oxygen from the air. Some amphibians, like the Bufo toad you might find in Florida, add poison to their mucus so they're no good to eat — not that people eat lots of toads in the first place!

Frog Babies

If you live near a pond you can even watch tadpoles growing up. Take a big, clean jar down to the pond. Look around for clear, round frogs' eggs floating in bunches on the edge of the water. Carefully scoop up about ten eggs in your jar, and fill it with pond water.

When you get home pour the water and the frog eggs into a bigger jar or an empty fish tank. Now you have to take care of them. Tadpoles are just babies, you know! Keep the tank in a shady place, so it feels like the edge of the pond.

If you don't have a fish tank filter, change the water in the tank every two days. You can use the same water from the pond where you found the eggs. Or, if you don't want to walk back and forth, fill a jar with water from your sink and let it sit outside for a night. That way the water is natural and safe for the frog babies to live in.

Frog eggs hatch into tadpoles after several days. Feed them bits of weeds from the pond where they came from, or chop up some leafy vegetables into very small pieces. Some tadpoles even eat tiny scraps of raw hamburger!

As tadpoles grow up you see their legs appear. Their tails shrink while their jumping legs grow longer and stronger. Their tiny gills will disappear, to be replaced by lungs (on the inside). This is almost like watching fish turn into amphibians, ready to move from the water to the land!

When the tadpoles are grown up into young frogs, take them back to the pond where they came from and let them swim away. (Otherwise you'll soon have hungry frogs jumping all over your house!)

Thick-skinned

About 300 million years ago a tough new bunch of animals first lumbered through the forests: the reptiles. Reptiles eventually ruled the earth for the whole Mesozoic era, over 150 million years. More important, some early reptiles were the ancestors of all birds and mammals, including us.

Reptiles look different from amphibians as soon as they hatch. For one thing, they come out of their eggs fully shaped, even if they aren't fully grown. Baby reptiles don't have to lose their tails and grow legs like tadpoles. And for another thing, reptiles don't hatch in water. They come out on dry land.

They can do that because reptiles lay a better grade of eggs. They aren't soft and squishy like amphibian eggs. If amphibian or fish eggs are taken out of the water, they dry up and the babies inside die. But a reptile egg has a tough leathery shell and built-in food and water supplies. It's like a little house with everything that the baby needs to grow. And because they have tough shells, reptile eggs can become fossils.

Just as reptiles put thick shells around their babies, they also put thick hides on themselves. Amphibians have soft, slimy skin, but reptiles have tough, dry scales, good for protecting themselves in the forests. One kind of reptile evolved with a hard shell to cover its body. That worked so well that turtles are still around today, 220 million years after they first evolved. Not bad for a slowpoke!

The Naked Egg

Here's how you can get a peek inside an egg without breaking the shell.

You will need
- a raw chicken egg
- a glass of vinegar
- a glass of water
- a spoon

Take a raw chicken egg from the fridge and let it sit in a glass of vinegar for one day. You will need to place a spoon on top of the egg to make sure it stays submerged in the vinegar.

Vinegar is a sour-smelling acid that dissolves the eggshell but leaves the inside of the egg intact. The bubbles you will see in the vinegar are signs that the shell is dissolving. When the shell is completely dissolved, carefully take the egg out of the cup and examine it.

Squeeze the egg gently to find out how it feels. If you squeeze too hard the egg will feel goopy — because it'll break all over your hand! Just squeeze it gently, and feel it bounce back. It's squishy but tough, sort of how a leathery-skinned reptile egg feels.

What do you see through the skin of the egg? Mostly clear liquid, the white of the egg, which is the baby's water supply. You can also spot the yellow yolk, the baby's food. But there's probably no baby for you to see. Supermarkets try not to sell eggs with embryos inside.

If you want to keep your naked egg to show your friends, store it safely in a glass of water. Then wash the vinegar smell off your hands.

The Oldest Trees

The oldest tree in the world is a bristlecone pine in California, which has been living for about 4,600 years. It's the oldest thing alive. But the oldest kinds of trees still living go back much further — 360 million years! They're called conifers, cycads, and ginkgos.

The reason these trees survived for so long is that they came up with a new way of reproducing. First they make pollen. The pollen cells drift through the air until they catch onto other cells still on trees and fertilize them. Then, instead of dropping the fertilized cells on the ground to fend for themselves, these trees build a little home for each cell, with all the food and water it needs to start growing. That little home is a seed. With their tough skin and their built-in water supply, seeds are the plant versions of reptile eggs.

The conifer family includes pine, fir, hemlock, yew, and spruce trees. You probably have a conifer tree or shrub right in your neighborhood. They're also called evergreens, because they keep their green needles all through the winter.

Cycads are much more rare than conifers, but there are still some in Florida, called sago palms because they look like palm trees. Ginkgos don't grow in the wild anymore, but you might find a pollen-making ginkgo planted in a park. If you want to find a ginkgo with seeds, go to a big arboretum and just follow your nose. They smell awful!

CONIFERS

FIR   SPRUCE   YEW   HEMLOCK   BRISTLECONE PINE

CYCADS

SAGO PALM

GINKGOS

FOSSILIZED

The Age of Reptiles

The Mesozoic era, from 240 million years ago to 65 million years ago, has a more exciting name: the Age of Reptiles! In this glorious period, huge reptiles, including the dinosaurs, evolved and ruled the earth. Some reptiles took to the skies. Others went back to conquer the oceans. For 140 million years dinosaurs dominated life on land.

The word dinosaur means "terrible lizard," but the first dinosaurs weren't very terrifying at all. They were rather small when they started out about 200 million years ago.

One early meat-eating dinosaur was *Coelophysis*. It stood about 4 feet (120 cm) high on its back legs, and ate any animal small enough to stuff into its mouth. One *Coelophysis* fossil has been found with smaller *Coelophysis* bones in its stomach. You'd have to be very hungry to eat your own little brother!

The biggest early dinosaur was *Plateosaurus*. It was 25 feet (8 m) long, with big flat feet and a long tail and neck. *Plateosaurus* traveled in herds, eating leaves and plants that grew near the ground. They could walk on either two legs or four, depending on how full their stomachs were.

At this time there were other reptiles bigger than the dinosaurs, and both *Coelophysis* and *Plateosaurus* had to beware of them. *Rutiodon* was one of these dangerous reptiles, a meat-eater 20 feet (6 m) long. It looked like a crocodile, but its nostrils were on the top of its head. A strong *Rutiodon* could kill a *Plateosaurus* for dinner and gulp down a *Coelophysis* for dessert.

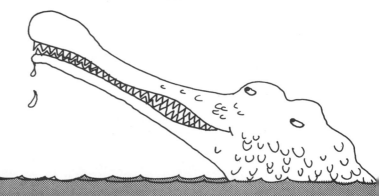

The Great

In only 60 million years, dinosaurs became the biggest, strongest, and fiercest animals living on earth. In fact, some dinosaurs were the biggest, strongest, and fiercest animals that lived on land at any time. But some of them were also small, weak, and peaceful. There were as many different kinds of dinosaurs as there are different kinds of animals today.

ROCKS!

Brachiosaurus was probably the heaviest animal ever to live on land. It weighed more than 85 tons (77 MT). That's as much as 15 elephants. *Brachiosaurus* measured 40 feet (12 m) high from the bottom of its huge front legs to the nostrils on top of its head. Natural selection allowed it to grow because nibbling leaves off the tops of the trees was a great way to make a living.

But first *Brachiosaurus* swallowed some rocks. That's not as dumb as it sounds. *Brachiosaurus* had no teeth to chew with, so it gulped its leaves down whole, and the rocks in its stomach ground up the leaves so that they could be digested. How would you like a nice granite appetizer before dinner?

As huge as *Brachiosaurus* was, it really wasn't very dangerous. All it wanted was to eat its leaves in peace. The worse it could have done to you is accidentally step on you and squash you flat!

The Terrible

Deinonychus, on the other hand, was only 5 feet (1½ m) tall but very dangerous. Or perhaps we should say, "on the other claw," because *Deinonychus* means "terrible claw." *Deinonychus* was a meat-eater and one of the most dangerous hunters of its time. You wouldn't want to be caught anywhere nearby at dinnertime.

The weapons *Deinonychus* used were the 5-inch-long (13 cm) claws on its second toes. It could hold those toes up out of the way when it walked around, or stick them out when it wanted to gouge out somebody's flesh.

Deinonychus could run very fast and grab onto its prey with its strong front claws. Then it would kick with its terrible feet. And if that wasn't frightening enough, *Deinonychus* hunted in packs like wolves. A dozen or so would gang up on one big dinosaur and share the meal.

Neither Fish nor Fowl

At the same time that the dinosaur family ruled the land, some of their cousins ruled the sea and the sky. This was the Age of Reptiles, so if you didn't have scales, watch out!

In the ocean, the plesiosaurs looked a lot like the dinosaurs, but they had flippers instead of legs. The biggest one was called *Elasmosaurus*, and it grew 50 feet (15 m) long, but 30 feet (9 m) of that was neck. Some people think the Loch Ness Monster might be a plesiosaur!

Another family of reptiles ruling the ocean were ichthyosaurs, which means "fish lizard." *Ichthyosaurus* evolved to look like a fish, just as dolphins look like fish today, even though they're mammals. The animals look the same because they fill the same space, or niche, in nature.

There were other giant reptiles in the ocean, like *Mosasaurus*, a 30-foot-long (9 m) lizard with flippers, sharp teeth, and a big appetite. Or *Archelon*, a turtle designed a lot like sea turtles today, except that its shell was 10 feet (3 m) across. That's as big as a car.

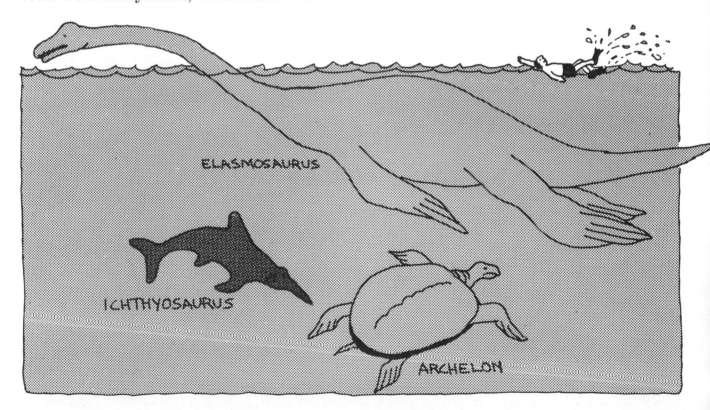

ELASMOSAURUS

ICHTHYOSAURUS

ARCHELON

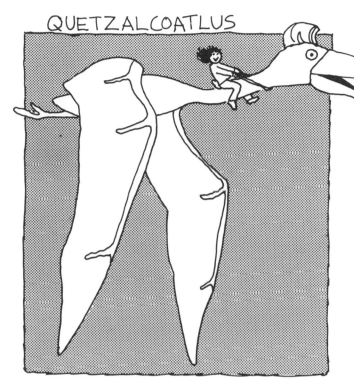

QUETZALCOATLUS

PEEP!

The pterodactyl family were the only reptiles that ever flew. Their wings were made of scales stretched over their long fingers. They probably had a thin coat of fur to keep them warm. When they weren't flying, they folded up their wings, looking a lot like bats.

Some pterodactyls were as small as pigeons, but another was 36 feet (11 m) across. Paleontologists named this giant *Quetzalcoatlus*, after a flying lizard in an ancient Mexican myth. It was the biggest thing that ever flew until we humans invented the airplane.

Another group of flying animals actually grew out of the dinosaur family. They all started with a creature called *Archaeopteryx*, whose scales had changed into feathers. Then their claws became smaller and they lost their teeth. Their bones became hollow, so they were lighter and could fly more easily. And their wings grew longer and stronger.

These dinosaur relations were the birds. That's right: birds are really just modified dinosaurs. And long after the dinosaurs died out the bird family is still going strong. That tiny chickadee singing outside your window is really a descendant of the dinosaurs!

Peep!

ARCHAEOPTERYX

Meet the Duckbills

After 100 million years of ruling the land, dinosaurs got pretty sophisticated. Some traveled and lived in family groups, a lot like we do.

Parasaurolophus families all lived around their nests. The mother probably sat on her eggs to keep them warm and safe. The father stalked around nearby and brought food back for her. And the *Parasaurolophus* youngsters played near the nest as well. Lots of nests were grouped together to make a dinosaur neighborhood.

Parasaurolophus might even have talked to each other, or at least trumpeted to each other like elephants. They had hollow bones sticking up 5 feet (1½ m) from their foreheads, and they could probably use these bones like trumpets to call one another. The sound could have traveled over many miles. How would you like your parents to call you home from a mile away?

Parasaurolophus came from a group of dinosaurs called the duckbills, because their skulls had flat mouths like ducks. Ducks don't have teeth, though, and *Parasaurolophus* had plenty of them to chew the pine needles they ate. Whenever one tooth wore out another grew in its place. One *Parasaurolophus* went through 2,000 teeth in its lifetime. That's enough visits from the tooth fairy to keep any parent busy!

Walking Tanks

By this time, the hunters had gotten bigger and stronger than ever, like our toothy friend *Tyrannosaurus*. Plant-eating dinosaurs had to evolve so that they could be safe from hungry meat-eaters.

The best protection against teeth and claws was strong armor, and many dinosaurs grew their own. *Ankylosaurus* was built like an army tank — and it grew even longer. It measured 25 feet (8 m) from its hard flat head to the bony lump on the end of its tail. When *Ankylosaurus* crouched low to the ground and swung its tail like a club, no hunter could get close enough to hurt it.

One of the last dinosaurs to evolve was *Torosaurus*, a close relative of *Triceratops*. The skull of *Torosaurus* was 10 feet (3 m) long, and it had horns that stuck out 2 feet (60 cm) over its eyes. The huge crest from its forehead protected almost half its back. From the front, *Torosaurus* was almost invincible.

Torosaurus probably traveled in packs for that reason. When danger threatened, the adults could stand in a circle with their horns out, and the young *Torosaurus* were safe in the middle of the circle. No *Tyrannosaurus*, no matter how hungry, would try fighting a whole herd of *Torosaurus*.

Say It with Flowers

Dinosaurs were certainly the main event back when they stalked the earth. We usually don't think much about the plants they were munching on, and don't realize that those plants were evolving too. We also don't think much about the things that would be missing from an early dinosaur landscape. Things like flowers and fruit and leafy trees such as oaks and maples. These plants were missing because they hadn't yet evolved.

But the big news 150 million years ago in the plant world, and in the world of dinosaur cuisine as well, was a new kind of plant. They spread like wildfire — or like wildflowers, actually. They were the first flowering plants, the ancestors of all modern flowers, all fruits, and all the trees that lose their leaves each winter.

Conifers, which already had been around for 150 million years when the new trees appeared, make huge amounts of pollen to make sure their seeds get fertilized. The more pollen there is, the more likely that some will fall in the right place and start a seed growing. The conifer forests where *Camptosaurus* camped out 140 million years ago were covered with a layer of pollen dust every spring. It's a good thing *Camptosaurus* didn't have hay fever!

Flowering plants evolved with a better way to spread their pollen. Instead of releasing thousands of pollen grains in the air, many flowers trick animals into carrying a bit of pollen from plant to plant. The carriers are mostly insects looking for food. They stop off on flowers for a sip of nectar and wind up going away with their legs covered with pollen, which rubs off on the next flower.

The more attractive a plant was, the more likely an insect would visit it and the easier its seeds would get fertilized. Flowers grew colorful, to catch the insect's eye, and fragrant, to catch the nose. They made sugary nectar, which insects liked to eat so much that they kept coming back.

After a flower's seeds are fertilized, the flower can grow into a fruit. Fruits provide seeds with food to grow and with a covering to protect them. They also provide food for dinosaurs, birds, mammals, and us. Apples and peaches are big and luscious because the trees benefit if you eat their fruit. As you eat them you carry away the seeds and eventually they end up on the ground, where they might grow into new plants. Think about that the next time you accidentally swallow a watermelon seed!

Were Dinosaurs Dumb?

You wouldn't dare call a 20-foot-long (6 m) *Triceratops* "stupid," even if you could. But for a long time paleontologists thought that all dinosaurs were slow and stupid, and that's why they became extinct so easily. They imagined dinosaurs lumbering along, eating leaves and occasionally each other, until they died and fell into the mud. Now paleontologists are beginning to think that many dinosaurs were actually pretty smart.

There were two main reasons why paleontologists thought dinosaurs were dumb. The first is that some dinosaurs had very small brains. The brain of a *Stegosaurus* was the same size as a walnut, even though the animal was 20 feet (6 m) long. One dinosaur was even named *Pachycephalosaurus*, or "thick-headed lizard." Its skull was 10 inches (25 cm) thick, thicker than your entire head. *Pachycephalosaurus* probably fought each other by butting skull against skull. Nobody would call that smart.

The other reason paleontologists thought dinosaurs were dumb was that they were supposed to be cold-blooded, and cold-blooded animals can't think as well as warm-blooded animals, like us.

Dinosaurs are really halfway between warm and cold. On one side, their relatives the lizards and crocodiles are cold-blooded. On the other side, their relatives the birds are warm-blooded. But because dinosaurs were built more like lizards, everybody assumed they were cold-blooded, too.

Now paleontologists think some of the dinosaurs were warm-blooded. One clue is that paleontologists have found blood vessels in the bones of some dinosaurs. Warm-blooded animals have blood vessels like those found in these dinosaurs, and cold-blooded animals don't. So perhaps some dinosaurs were warm-blooded and labelled cold-blooded by mistake. Wouldn't that make your blood boil?

But the best evidence that dinosaurs weren't stupid is how long they ruled the earth: over 140 million years. Dinosaurs who hunted for their food were probably as smart and active as modern-day lions — and too intelligent for them all to die out at once, unless something terrible happened to their world.

Gone!

Sixty-five million years ago the temperature of the air turned a little cooler than before. It wasn't suddenly cold, as if the temperature had dropped to freezing overnight. The average temperature we're used to today is only about 8°F (5°C) cooler than what the dinosaurs enjoyed. But those few degrees mean a lot.

What did the dinosaurs think of all this? You couldn't have found a dinosaur to ask. Not even one. They weren't just hiding. (It would be very hard for a 70-foot-long (21 m) *Alamosaurus* to hide.) They had all died out. Sixty-five million years ago, all the dinosaurs in the world became extinct.

At the same time the dinosaurs all disappeared, so did their cousins the plesiosaurs, the ichthyosaurs, and the pterodactyls. The only close relatives to the dinosaur that are alive today are crocodiles and birds.

Many other kinds of animals also died out at the same time. Ammonites, which were relatives of squids, became extinct. Rudists, huge clams that formed reefs in the shallow oceans, all died off. This was a time of mass extinction, and the dinosaurs were unlucky enough to be caught in it.

The biggest mystery that paleontologist detectives have to solve is what caused this mass extinction. If we can answer that question, then we solve the disappearance of the dinosaurs.

Meteors and Meat-eaters

Meteors are also called "shooting stars," and you can see a lot of them at night in August. Usually meteors burn up in the air because they're moving so fast, but when one reaches the earth's surface it's called a *meteorite*. Small meteorites hit the earth all the time, and nobody has ever died from one. But what would happen if a huge meteorite, 6 miles (10 km) across, smashed into the earth? Nothing good, that's for sure. Some scientists think that a meteorite caused the mass extinction that killed the dinosaurs.

A meteorite that large would smash into the ground in a tremendous collision. The explosion of that meteorite hitting the earth would throw huge clouds of dirt and dust into the air. Those dust clouds would block out the sun for several years. Plants don't grow without sunlight, so there would be fewer plants in the world. So much of life depends on plants for food that many animals would start to die. Plant-eating dinosaurs would starve to death. After the big plant-eaters died, the meat-eating dinosaurs wouldn't have anything to eat either, and they would die off, too. Soon there wouldn't be any dinosaurs left.

There is one clue that a meteorite really did hit the earth 65 millions years ago. Geologists have found a thin layer of clay loaded with the metal *iridium* laid down in many places around the world just as dinosaurs and other creatures disappeared. Iridium is very rare. Most of it is found deep inside the earth — and in meteorites!

Going, Going . . .

The problem is that the dinosaurs didn't all die suddenly in a huge explosion. It took thousands and thousands of years for them to become extinct. But when you're thinking about millions and millions of years, as paleontologists do, even a thousand years seem like a very short time.

The truth is that many animals were in trouble before 65 million years ago. There weren't as many kinds of dinosaurs as there had been. Other creatures, like the ichthyosaurs and the ammonites, were already dying. The environment was in a very fragile state.

Perhaps there were volcanic explosions huge enough to spread iridium from inside the earth all around. Perhaps a meteorite did strike the earth. It didn't have to be 6 miles across to do damage. All that was needed was a little problem.

Remember that temperatures all over the world dropped a few degrees. That's not much, but that changed the world a lot. Animals and plants that needed a very warm climate became extinct after several hundred years of cold. Perhaps the animals that were adapted for colder air, like furry mammals and feathered birds, were better able to survive and spread.

So even if dinosaurs were the biggest and strongest animals ever, they could still be killed by a little change in temperature.

What If?

Most paleontologists are a little sad that the dinosaurs all died out. We'll never get a chance to see one in the flesh, to find out if they really looked and acted as we think they did. But mostly we're glad that dinosaurs aren't still around, lurking in the woods, hunting for paleontologists to eat.

We're glad for another reason as well. The disappearance of the dinosaurs meant that other kinds of animals had room to evolve. Especially mammals! They grew bigger, now that they didn't have to hide from dinosaur hunters. They had more food to eat, since the dinosaurs weren't swallowing everything first. And eventually they took over the world, just as the dinosaurs had.

What if the dinosaurs hadn't died out? They and their relatives would still be in charge of the earth. Mammals couldn't have come out from under the bushes where they were hiding. Humans would never have evolved. Maybe reptile people, descended from the dinosaurs, might be walking around instead!

Mammal Time

Around the time of the first dinosaurs another important new gang of animals appeared. They had evolved from long-legged, toothy creatures called *therapsids*.

The therapsids had discovered that they could have the far northern and southern parts of Pangaea all to themselves if they could only keep warm. First they ruffled up their reptile scales for insulation. After millions of years, those scales grew thinner and softer, until they turned into hair. That helped the therapsids keep pretty warm.

The next important change for the therapsids was to become warm-blooded. Warm-blooded means that an animal's blood keeps its body at a constant temperature. Humans always have a temperature of about 98.6°F (37°C) unless they're sick. Cold-blooded animals get their heat from the sun, so their temperatures go up and down depending on the last time they sat out in the sun. Warm-blooded animals have to eat more food, but they can stay warm in cold places.

Eventually, as therapsids became furry and warm-blooded, their descendants evolved into mammals. Mammals are the only animals today with fur. Even the rhinoceros has hair: that's what its horn is made of! Most mammals give birth to live babies instead of laying eggs. Then mommy mammals can feed their babies with milk made in their bodies. But one of the best things about mammals is you! You and all

other humans, all dogs and cats, horses, bats, and dolphins are mammals.

Like the dinosaurs, mammals started out small. But when the dinosaurs grew larger, the mammals stayed small. Otherwise the dinosaurs would eat them! For over 100 million years mammals hid under bushes and came out only at night, when most dinosaurs were asleep. That wasn't a very good start for our ancestors, was it?

But then, out went the dinosaurs, in came the mammals! That's what it looks like, anyway. Instead of huge vegetarian dinosaurs, we find big, lumbering, plant-eating mammals. And right beside them, eating the plant-eaters, was a fresh batch of carnivores, also mammals. All the reptiles' ways of making a living — attacking, grazing, plucking leaves — were taken over by mammals about 65 million years ago. But remember, our ancestors had to wait for the dinosaurs to go extinct before they got the chance to rule the land.

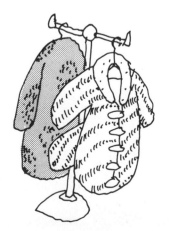

Our Nearest Relatives

Who are your closest relatives? Your parents? Your kid sister? Sure. But all humans are related to each other. We all belong to the same species. Our scientific name is *Homo sapiens*, which means "wise human." Judging from all the wars, pollution, and other problems we have, we're not so wise all the time. But we earn our name because we can think, and as far as we know, no other animals can think like we do.

One thing we can think about is our closest relatives in the animal world. Can you guess? It's not too hard, because if you've ever watched chimpanzees at a zoo you probably thought they acted almost human (at least as human as your kid sister). Chimps play and make faces at each other. Their bodies — arms and legs, hands and feet — look a lot like ours, though chimps are much hairier than we are.

Chimpanzees are great apes, like gorillas, orangutans, and gibbons. Apes are different from monkeys because they have no tails. Monkeys are also our relatives, but a little bit further removed. Even further back in our family tree come lemurs and tarsiers. All of us together make up the *Primates*, or "first," order of mammals.

You can be proud of your ancestors. Primates go back into dinosaur times. Our early ancestors were scurrying around while *Tyrannosaurus* was looking for its dinner. And after the dinosaurs died out, primates grew larger and wiser.

Lucy and the Fossil People

It's great to find a brachiopod, a trilobite, or a clam. It's a thrill to stumble on a dinosaur skull poking out of the hillside. But imagine the excitement of going out and finding traces of our ancient ancestors preserved right alongside the bones of hippos, elephants, and antelopes!

Sometime around 5 million years ago our family tree split off from the great apes. Some of the oldest fossil humans found so far — *Australopithecus* creatures, like the famous fossil specimen named Lucy, from Ethiopia — look very much like chimpanzees. They could stand up straight, though, and maybe were just a bit smarter than modern-day chimps.

AUSTRALOPITHECUS

Thrice the Rice

There are a couple of ways we can check human fossils to get an idea how smart our ancestors really were. For one thing, we can measure how big their brains were by the size of their hollow skulls. Scientists estimate brain size by filling skulls with uncooked rice, and then dumping the rice out into a large measuring cup. (Try it the next time you want to measure a container with an odd shape.)

Those oldest human fossils like Lucy turn out to be just a little brainier than modern-day chimps; less than 1⅔ cups (400 cc) of rice or brain could fit into their heads. In comparison, the skulls of modern human adults can hold almost 6 cups (1400 cc) of rice. Even the brain of a ten-year-old kid takes up about 5½ cups (1300 cc) of space.

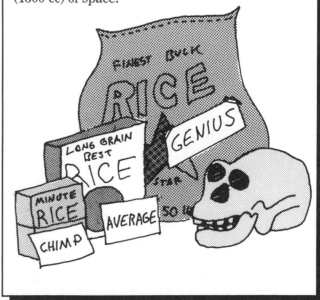

Standing Tall

As we climb up the rocks that have human fossils, we get closer and closer to our modern times. And the fossils look more and more like us. After the Lucy types, the next important step was the appearance of *Homo erectus* about 2 million years ago. These people had bigger brains than Lucy but smaller brains than we have — about 4 cups (1000 cc) worth. For the first time our ancestors spread from Africa and started living in Europe and Asia as well.

Another way we know *erectus* people were smarter is that *archeologists* have found their tools. Archeologists, like paleontologists, dig up ancient things. But archeologists go after human-made objects, or *artifacts*. The smarter people are, in general, the more complicated their artifacts are likely to be. Lucy and her pals didn't leave any tools behind, so they couldn't have been very far along the path to high technology.

But the *erectus* people knew how to make simple tools out of wood and stone. We've found many of their artifacts, especially

HOMO ERECTUS

HOMO ERECTUS TOOLS

hand axe

pointed hand axe

knife

choppers and axes. The toolmakers chipped stones into the shapes they needed by pounding or pushing one rock against another. It took hours to make one simple scraper! These old tools are even more common in the archeological deposits than bones are.

People evolved while glaciers were coming and going, covering huge parts of Europe, then melting back, then covering everything up again. During the last big ice attack, people known as Neanderthals lived in Europe. They had brains as big as ours, or even slightly larger. And they could make a large variety of stone tools.

But the Neanderthals disappeared about 35,000 years ago. Why is still a mystery, one that paleontologists and anthropologists still haven't completely solved. Did the Neanderthals become extinct? Or did they evolve into modern Europeans?

One important clue is that modern *Homo sapiens* (that's us) evolved about 100,000 years ago in Africa. We started to spread to other places about 50,000 years ago. Our bones show up in Europe about 35,000 years ago — just as the Neanderthals disappeared. At the same time the many different kinds of stone tools we could make replaced the Neanderthal tools. *Homo sapiens* artists even started to paint the walls of their caves.

What do you think? Did we take over Europe from the Neanderthals, and maybe make them go extinct? Or did we evolve from Neanderthals? There's something to put your 5½ cups of brain to!

BOW WOW!

HOMO SAPIENS

Land of the Giants

The mammals who ruled North America 15,000 years ago grew to giant size, just like the dinosaurs after they had been around for a few million years. These Ice Age mammals were larger than any animals on the continent today.

One cool cat from the Ice Age, *Smilodon*, is also called a saber-toothed tiger because it had two long, curved teeth, like swords, and because it was as large as a tiger. Those teeth were too big and too sharp for chewing. Instead *Smilodon* used them to stab animals so that they bled to death. *Smilodon* was the most fearsome hunter on the continent for thousands of years.

You can tell that *Smilodon* wasn't an ancestor of your pet cat by looking at its teeth. Saber-tooth cats had long pointed teeth in the top of their mouth and small teeth on the bottom. But if you look in your cat's mouth you can see that the pointed teeth are the same size on top and bottom. There aren't any saber-toothed species left — thank goodness!

The giant ground sloth was a peaceful leaf-eater. But the plants it ate were 16 feet (5 m) off the ground! Some ground sloth hair that was preserved shows that it had shaggy red-brown fur. It weighed 5 tons (4½ MT), which to *Smilodon* meant only one thing:

plenty of meat! Smaller sloths are living today in South America, where they hang upside-down from trees.

Teratornis is the big name of a huge vulture. Its wings measured at least 12 feet (3½ m) across, and it probably weighed 50 pounds (23 kg). It may have been the biggest flying bird ever. *Teratornis* was a meat-eater, but it didn't hunt its own food. It circled around in the air or sat on tree branches waiting for a hunter like *Smilodon* to kill a ground sloth. When the hunter had eaten its fill, *Teratornis* pecked the rest of the food off the bones.

The strangest creature in Ice Age America was called *Glyptodon*. It had thick, armored skin all over its 9-foot-long (3 m) body, like its modern relative the armadillo. On the end of its tail was a spiky ball that it could use to club predators, if it needed to. But *Glyptodon* was probably too tough for most hunters to eat.

All these animals became extinct about 11,000 years ago, just as the glaciers were beginning to melt. It wasn't a mass extinction, because smaller animals did not die out at the same time. Some paleontologists say a new mammal came to North America and hunted down all the others. But who could have killed these giants?

The First Americans

Here's the suspect! Do these animals look familiar? They should, because they're us — *Homo sapiens*. Humans are the mammals that some scientists think were partly responsible for killing off the giant animals of North America.

Humans journeyed from Asia into North America as the last great Ice Age was winding down. They came by walking! The ice of the glaciers used up so much water that the oceans were at a much lower level than they are today. In fact, they were too low to cover the area between Alaska and Siberia. That space was all land, so people could walk across. Now Asia and North America are separated by a narrow body of seawater called the Bering Strait.

These first travelers became the native people of North and South America. They probably followed herds of migrating animals, such as reindeer or elk, which they hunted for food. Spear points have been found stuck into the bones of extinct species of buffalo, so we know these early Americans must have been good hunters.

In fact, it's the stone arrowheads, spear points, scrapers, and knives that give us our best clues to the way of life of these first Americans. Even today, in farm fields and along river banks, kids can get lucky and find these stony points and arrowheads. Usually they're not too old, going back to tribes living in the area one or two hundred years ago. But some of these artifacts are thousands of years old.

Later many tribes turned to farming instead of hunting. In the American Southwest, where the dry conditions preserved delicate cloth, ropes, and baskets, the archeological record is really rich. Farming tribes built big houses high up on cliff faces, where they could escape from their enemies by scaling up tall ladders. These early farmers also left behind thousands of clay pots, which they probably used to store food. By that time, there were no more large Ice Age mammals to hunt.

Could humans really have wiped out the huge mastodons, mammoths, woolly rhinos, and giant sloths? In the last century, Americans coming from Europe hunted the bison almost to extinction. Hunting also helped kill off all the passenger pigeons. So we know that humans, with their intelligence and weapons, can destroy animal species.

But hunting can't be the whole story. Remember that dinosaurs and lots of other animals and plants, large and small, went extinct long before there were any people around to hunt them. Changes in climate almost always turn out to be the most important suspect in an extinction mystery. Probably, as the last of the ice sheets retreated north, the environment of North America had changed so much that it was just too difficult for many large animals to live there. But it was fine for people!

Future Humans

Where, oh where, did they ever dream up E.T.? Why does he look so skinny, with a fragile, almost useless body and that huge head, with the big bulging brain inside?

E.T. is not unique. Almost always, when science fiction writers imagine aliens from outer space who are smarter than we are, they come up with something like E.T. Why?

E.T. looks a lot like what many scientists have guessed future humans will look like. After all, they say, our fossil history shows that people's brains got bigger as they evolved. And because people rely more and more on machines to do their work for them, some scientists have decided that our bodies will sort of waste away in the future. We'll need only our minds, so they'll get bigger and bigger, and we won't need our bodies, so they'll shrivel up. Just like E.T.

What do you think? Here's a hint that the science fiction gang hasn't thought about very much. Fossil bones show the ancient species in our family didn't change much once they first appeared. The *erectus* species lived all over Africa, Asia, and Europe for at least 1½ million years, and didn't change.

GREAT GREAT GREAT GREAT GREAT GRANPA

There are over 5,000 million people on earth right now. For the whole species to change into something as different as E.T. is very unlikely.

So what's the best guess about what future people will look like? If our species avoids extinction — by not blowing ourselves up, for instance — we'll probably go on looking pretty much the same as we do now.

Not that things will always be exactly the same. Far from it! We'll continue to learn about new things, to use our brains to solve big problems, like feeding everyone on the planet and getting more energy for heat and transportation. That's our evolutionary future in a nutshell: thinking up exciting new technologies like space travel, superconductivity, and ice cream that never melts. The sky's the limit as far as human ingenuity and braininess are concerned!

Homo sapiens seem to have started in Africa, and then spread to Europe and Asia, to Australia and the Pacific islands by boat, and at last to North and South America by land. Now there are even a few humans living on Antarctica, the last continent on earth. Where will *Homo sapiens* go next? Under the ocean? To other planets in the solar system?

Appendix I: Time Line

It's hard enough to keep track of all the different plants and animals that lived during the last 3,500 million years. When we start thinking about all the changes that have taken place on the earth too . . . good grief! We know that dinosaurs were alive and well 100 million years ago. But where was North America drifting off to? What were the mammals doing? How was the weather? Were there butterflies in the air? And what kind of fish were swimming in the sea?

If we think about these things at all we usually think about them separately. But on the *time line* that follows, we've tried to spread out the whole history of everything: the continents and climate, plants and animals, land and sea.

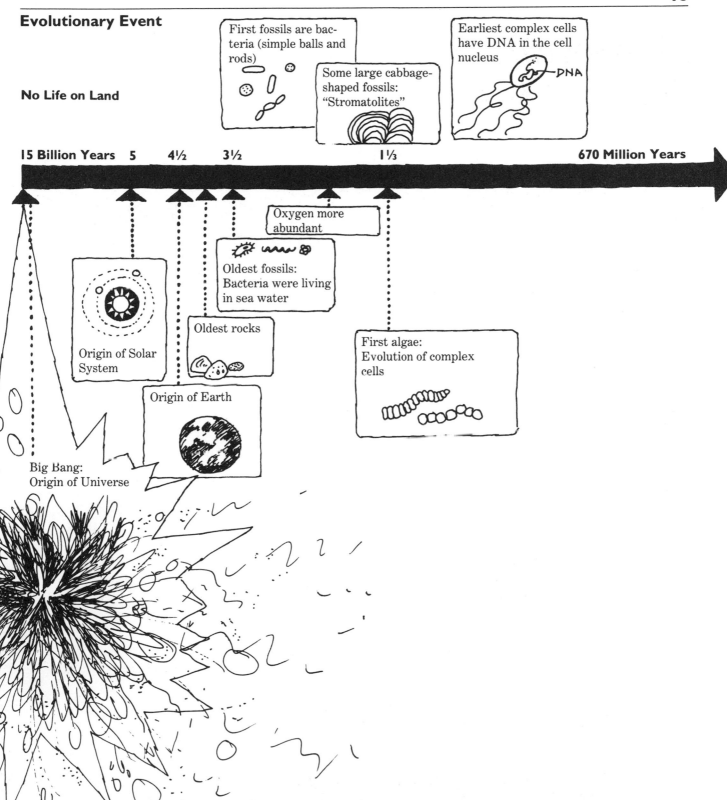

Evolutionary Event

First fossils are bacteria (simple balls and rods)

Earliest complex cells have DNA in the cell nucleus

DNA

Some large cabbage-shaped fossils: "Stromatolites"

No Life on Land

15 Billion Years   5   4½   3½   1⅓   670 Million Years

Oxygen more abundant

Oldest fossils: Bacteria were living in sea water

Origin of Solar System

Oldest rocks

First algae: Evolution of complex cells

Origin of Earth

Big Bang: Origin of Universe

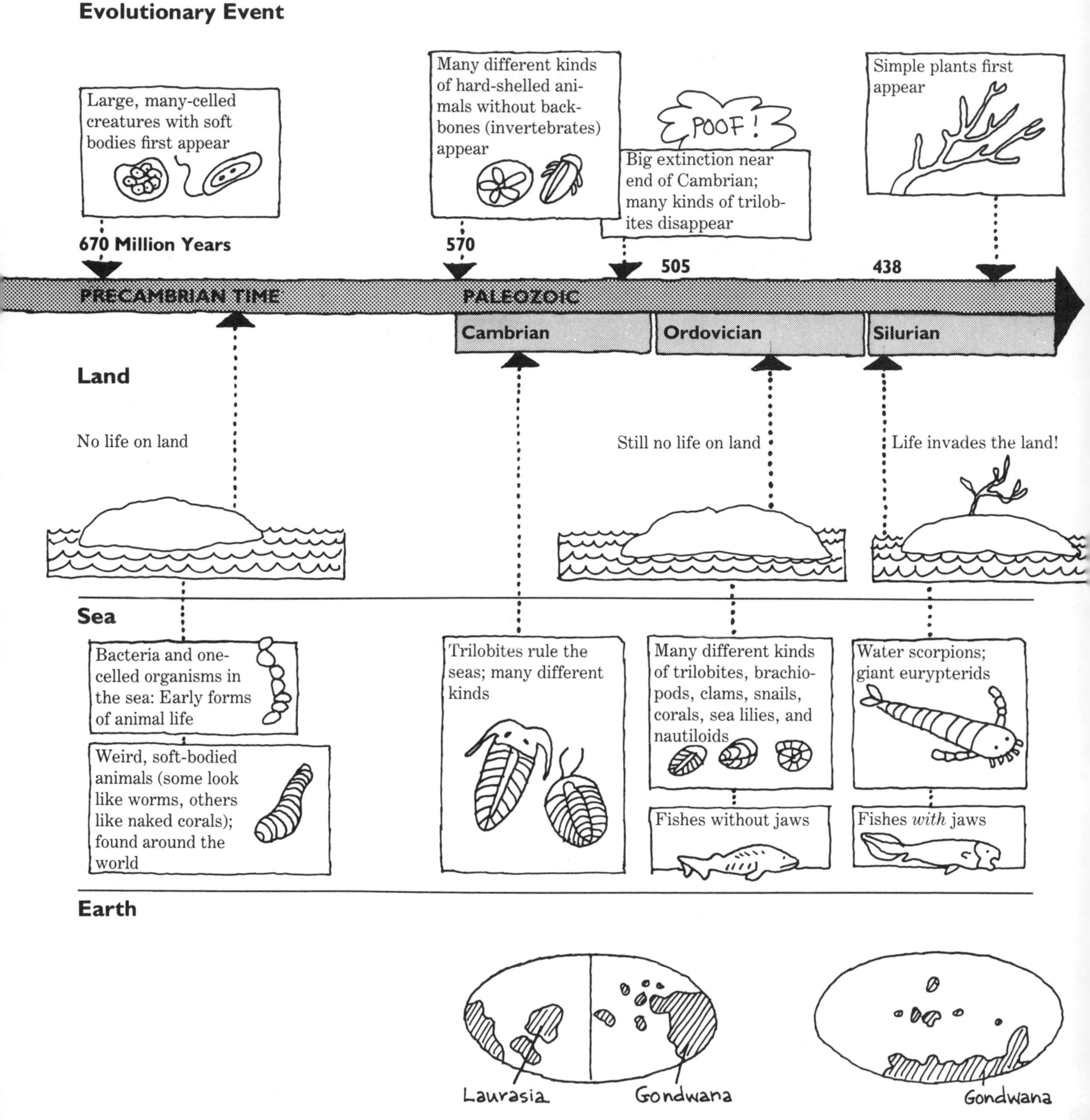

Evolutionary Event

Large, many-celled creatures with soft bodies first appear

Many different kinds of hard-shelled animals without backbones (invertebrates) appear

POOF!

Big extinction near end of Cambrian; many kinds of trilobites disappear

Simple plants first appear

670 Million Years

570

505

438

PRECAMBRIAN TIME

PALEOZOIC

Cambrian

Ordovician

Silurian

Land

No life on land

Still no life on land

Life invades the land!

Sea

Bacteria and one-celled organisms in the sea: Early forms of animal life

Weird, soft-bodied animals (some look like worms, others like naked corals); found around the world

Trilobites rule the seas; many different kinds

Many different kinds of trilobites, brachiopods, clams, snails, corals, sea lilies, and nautiloids

Fishes without jaws

Water scorpions; giant eurypterids

Fishes *with* jaws

Earth

Laurasia   Gondwana

Gondwana

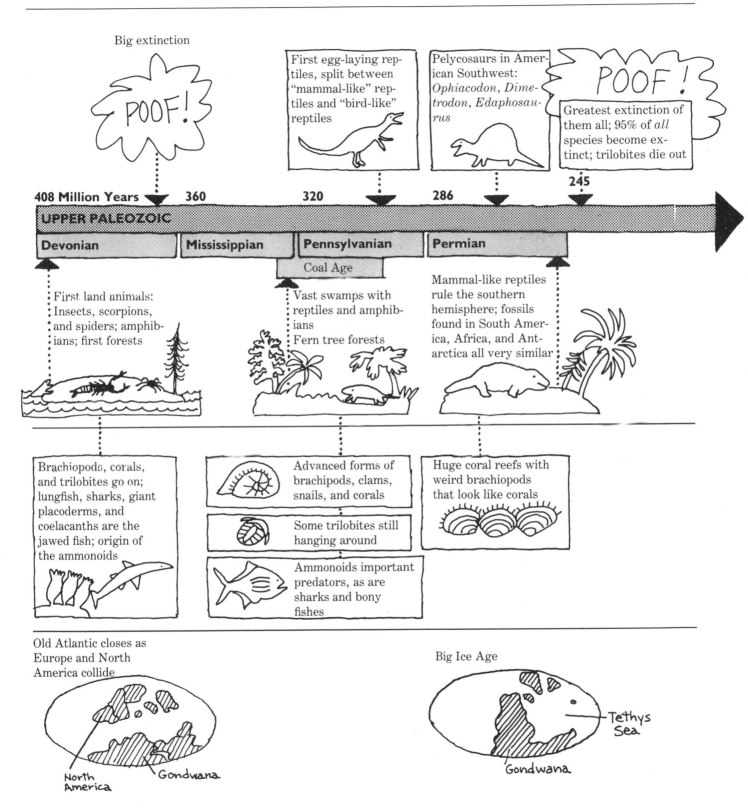

Big extinction

POOF!

First egg-laying reptiles, split between "mammal-like" reptiles and "bird-like" reptiles

Pelycosaurs in American Southwest: *Ophiacodon*, *Dimetrodon*, *Edaphosaurus*

POOF!

Greatest extinction of them all; 95% of *all* species become extinct; trilobites die out

408 Million Years   360   320   286   245

UPPER PALEOZOIC

Devonian   Mississippian   Pennsylvanian   Permian

Coal Age

First land animals: Insects, scorpions, and spiders; amphibians; first forests

Vast swamps with reptiles and amphibians
Fern tree forests

Mammal-like reptiles rule the southern hemisphere; fossils found in South America, Africa, and Antarctica all very similar

Brachiopods, corals, and trilobites go on; lungfish, sharks, giant placoderms, and coelacanths are the jawed fish; origin of the ammonoids

Advanced forms of brachiopods, clams, snails, and corals

Some trilobites still hanging around

Ammonoids important predators, as are sharks and bony fishes

Huge coral reefs with weird brachiopods that look like corals

Old Atlantic closes as Europe and North America collide

North America   Gondwana

Big Ice Age

Tethys Sea

Gondwana

Evolutionary Event

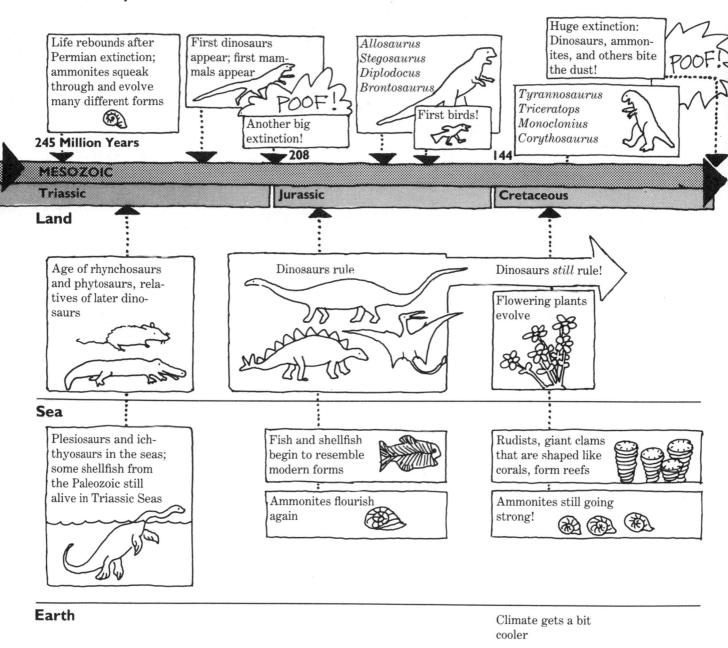

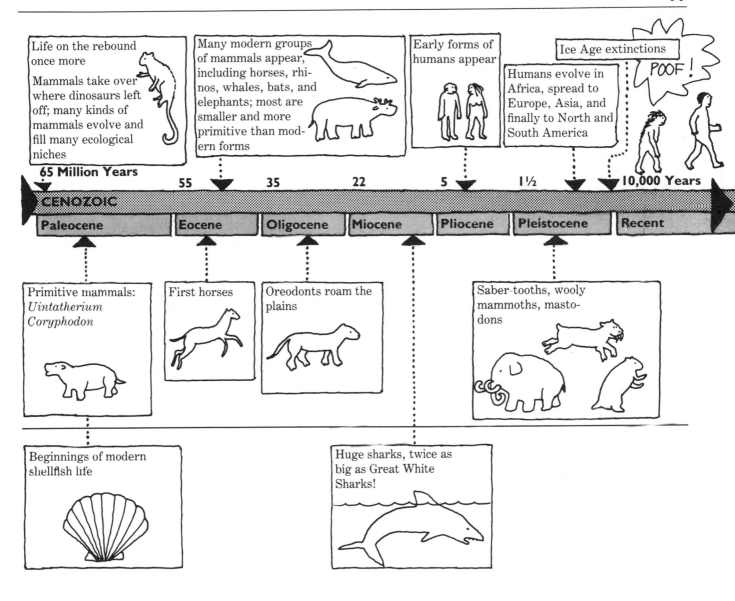

Life on the rebound once more

Mammals take over where dinosaurs left off; many kinds of mammals evolve and fill many ecological niches

65 Million Years

Many modern groups of mammals appear, including horses, rhinos, whales, bats, and elephants; most are smaller and more primitive than modern forms

Early forms of humans appear

Ice Age extinctions

Humans evolve in Africa, spread to Europe, Asia, and finally to North and South America

POOF!

55   35   22   5   1½   **10,000 Years**

CENOZOIC

Paleocene   Eocene   Oligocene   Miocene   Pliocene   Pleistocene   Recent

Primitive mammals: *Uintatherium* *Coryphodon*

First horses

Oreodonts roam the plains

Saber-tooths, wooly mammoths, mastodons

Beginnings of modern shellfish life

Huge sharks, twice as big as Great White Sharks!

Another big Ice Age: Glaciers cover upper half of North America four times

Appendix 2: Hunting on Holiday

Here are directions to 52 places in North America where you can see real fossils. With the right equipment and planning, you can start your own fossil collection. Just follow the guidelines in "Collecting Dos and Don'ts" to stay safe.

Because North America has changed so much since life began, some places are better for spotting fossils than others. Perhaps you and your family can check out different parts of the country when you're on vacation. And there are always the museums and national parks with fossil displays. We've included some in this list.

These fossil collecting places and many others are listed in the *Centennial Field Guide* of the Geological Society of America (Boulder, Colorado).

✳   collecting allowed
☞   tours or displays

WEST

California

✳   *San Diego area:* San Onofre State Beach.
Take Interstate 5, exit at Basilone Road, and follow the road southeast along the coast for 3.2 miles (5.1 km) to the beach entrance. Walk down to the trail from the parking lot to the beach.

There are marine invertebrate fossils from the Ice Age and earlier under the cliffs along the beach.

☞   *Los Angeles:* George C. Page Museum, next door to the La Brea Tar Pits.
Hancock Park, 5801 Wilshire Boulevard, Los Angeles, CA 90036. (213) 936-2230. Admission: $3 adults, $.75 kids, $1.50 senior citizens and students with identification. Admission the second Tuesday of every month is free. Hours: Tuesday–Sunday, 10:00 A.M.–5:00 P.M. Closed Mondays.

The museum holds over 1 million Ice Age fossils found in the tar pits nearby. In addition, it displays films, reconstructed mammoths and Dire Wolves, and a paleontology lab.

☞   *Los Angeles:* Museum of Natural History of Los Angeles County.
900 Exposition Boulevard, Los Angeles, CA 90000. (213) 744-3466. Admission: $3 adults, $.75 kids ages 5–12, $1.50 senior citizens and students with identification. Admission the first Tuesday of every month is free. Hours: Tuesday–Sunday, 10:00 A.M.–5:00 P.M. Closed Mondays.

Tyrannosaurus, saber-toothed cats, and the giant flightless bird *Diatryma* are found here.

✳   *Santa Cruz area:* Capitola, California.
Park your car on the south edge of Capitola and walk south along the Monterey Bay beach below the cliffs.

The rocks here are absolutely loaded with 3-million-year-old clams, snails, and other invertebrates, as well as whale and porpoise bones.

✳   *San Francisco:* Fort Funston reservation.
Use the oceanfront parking just west of the northern end of Lake Merced, or park in Fort Funston on Route 35. Follow trails to the beach.

You can easily find fossils of clams, snails, and especially sand dollars that are over 2 million years old.

☞   *San Francisco:* California Academy of Sciences.
10th Avenue and Fulton, Golden Gate Park, San Francisco, CA 94118. (415) 221-5100. Admission: $4 adults, $2 students ages 12–17 and senior citizens, $1 kids ages 6–11. Admission the first Wednesday of every month is free. Hours: 10:00 A.M.–5:00 P.M. every day. Open until 8:45 P.M. the first Wednesday of every month. Open every day until 7:00 P.M. from Independence Day to Labor Day.

The Life Through Time hall displays evolutionary history through videos, models, and dozens of fossils, including dinosaur skeletons and eggs.

☞   *Berkeley:* University of California Museum of Paleontology.
Earth Sciences Building, Hurst and Euclid Avenues, Berkeley, CA 94720. (415) 642-1821. Admission: Free.

Pick up pamphlets for self-guided tours in the lobby. Hours: Monday–Friday, 8:00 A.M.–5:00 P.M. Closed weekends.

This museum is mainly for professional paleontologists, but there are fine displays of *Dilophosaurus* and *Tyrannosaurus* fossils.

Oregon

☞ *John Day:* John Day Fossil Beds National Monument. Park headquarters are near the junction of U.S. Highways 395 and 26, at 420 West Main Street, John Day, OR 97845. (503) 987-2333. Hours: Monday–Friday, 8:00 A.M.–4:30 P.M. The Sheep Rock Visitor Center, the park's main exhibit area, is reached by turning north off U.S. Highway 26 onto Route 19, and driving 2 miles (3.2 km). It is open every day 8:30 A.M.–6:00 P.M., from mid-March through October.

Fossils from all epochs of the Ice Age have been found in John Day. The Island of Time Trail in the Sheep Rock Unit is a half-mile (.8 km) walk tracing the fossil history of the park.

Remember: Don't remove any fossils, rocks, or wildlife from national parks and monuments.

South Dakota

☞ *Interior:* Badlands National Park. The Cedar Pass Visitors Center is on Highway 240, which loops off Interstate 90 and through the park. Interior, SD 57750. (605) 433-5361. Admission: $3 per car, $1 per person ages 16–62 on buses. Admission is free from October to April. Hours: 8:00 A.M.–4:30 P.M., with extended hours in the summer.

Mammal fossils from 40 million years ago can be seen along the quarter-mile (.4 km) Fossil Exhibit Trail. During the summer paleontologists chat about the fossils as they study and preserve them.

Wyoming

☞ *Kemmerer:* Fossil Butte National Monument. The Monument is north of Highway 30, 11 miles (18 km) west of Kemmerer, past two quarries suitable for fossil hunting. Office on Central Avenue, Kemmerer, WY 83101-0527. (307) 877-4898. Hours: 8:30 A.M.–5:30 P.M. every day from May to September.

The fossils of fish that swam here 50 million years ago are the best in the U.S. But you should have seen the ones that got away!

SOUTHWEST

Arizona

✳ *Tucson area:* Dry Canyon, near the Mexican border. A trip for the adventurous: four-wheel-drive vehicles are recommended. Take Interstate 10 east to Arizona Route 90. After driving 13 miles (21 km) south on Route 90, turn right onto a dirt road at a ranch gate. You will cross public land for a few miles before arriving at Dry Canyon.

There are rocks between 500 million and 300 million years old with many invertebrate fossils exposed in the low hills on the sides of the canyon.

☞ *Holbrook:* Petrified Forest National Park. The 28-mile (45 km) driving trail through the park runs between Interstate 40 and U.S. Highway 180. Holbrook, AZ 86028. (602) 524-6228. Admission: $5 per car, or $2 per person arriving by bus, by bicycle, or on foot. Hours: Painted Desert Visitors Center open 8:00

A.M.–4:00 P.M. all year, with extended daylight hours in the summer.

The beautiful fossilized trees that give the park its name grew during the first part of the Mesozoic era, when the huge reptile phytosaur hunted early dinosaurs and other prey. The Rainbow Forest Museum in the south of the park has phytosaur skeleton and other fossils on display.

Colorado

☛ *Florissant:* Florissant Fossil Beds National Monument.
From Denver, take Interstate 25 south to Colorado Springs, and Route 24 west to Florissant, Colorado. Turn south toward Cripple Creek on Teller County Road #1, which is unpaved. The monument is half a mile (.8 km) south of town.

The site preserves the best plants from the early Cenozoic era yet discovered in North America.

☛ *Denver:* Denver Museum of Natural History.
City Park, 22nd Avenue and Colorado Boulevard, Denver, CO 80205. (303) 370-6363. Admissions: $4.00 adults, $2.00 kids and senior citizens. Hours: 9:00 A.M.–5:00 P.M. every day.

The fossil collection includes a very well preserved *Stegosaurus* and older fossils.

New Mexico

✳ *Albuquerque area:* Sandia Mountains.
Take Interstate 40 just 4 miles (6 km) east of the city limits. Look on the north side of the western lanes of Interstate 40.

There are marine invertebrate fossils from the late Paleozoic era embedded in these rocks.

Utah

✳ *Salt Lake City area:* Tucker, Utah.
Take Route 6 southeast. Stop at the roadside park just before arriving at the town of Tucker, and walk north to the nearby rock outcrops.

These rocks are actually giant lake deposits, with fish fossils, among others, from the early Cenozoic era.

☛ *Salt Lake City:* Utah Museum of Natural History, on the University of Utah campus off Highway 40. Follow the dinosaur tracks from Rice Stadium to the museum. Salt Lake City, UT 84112. (801) 581-4303. Admission: $3.50 adults, $1.50 kids ages 5–12. Hours: Monday–Friday, 1:00 P.M.–6:30 P.M.; Saturday, 10:00 A.M.–9:00 P.M.; Sunday, 12:00 noon–5:00 P.M.. In the summer the museum opens at 9:30 A.M. Monday through Saturday and closes at 9:00 P.M. Monday, Friday, and Saturday, and at 5:30 P.M. Tuesday through Thursday.

Among the skeletons exhibited here near dinosaur country are two *Allosaurus* and a *Camptosaurus*. A simulated quarry in the museum lets little kids learn how to dig for dinosaur bones as paleontologists do. (The quarry opens an hour after the museum and closes an hour before.)

Call ahead to museums and parks to make sure they'll be open when you want to visit.

☞ *Jensen:* Dinosaur National Monument.
Headquarters are on Interstate 40, 4 miles (6 km) east of the Utah border, in Colorado. Dinosaur, CO 81610. (303) 374-2216. The Dinosaur Quarry is 7 miles (11 km) north of Jensen, Utah. (801) 789-2115. Admission to the Quarry area. $5 per car, or $2 per person over age 16 on buses. Hours: 8:00 A.M.–4:30 P.M., with extended hours from spring through fall.

The Dinosaur Quarry displays over 2,200 fossil bones still in the rock where paleontologists found them. During summer months you can see people at work unearthing and preserving more specimens.

MIDWEST

Illinois

✳ *Chicago area:* Margery C. Carlson Nature Preserve.
Take Interstate 80 and highway 178 to Lowell. From Lowell, go ½ mile (.8 km) west along the south bank of the Vermilion River.

There are marine fossils on the bank here that are 300 million years old.

☞ *Chicago:* Field Museum of Natural History.
Roosevelt Road and Lake Shore Drive, Chicago, IL 60605. (312) 922-9410. Admission: $2 adults, $1 kids over age 6, $4 family rate. Hours: 9:00 A.M.–5:00 P.M.

This museum has a Fossil Hall, showing creatures from all eras of the earth's history. There are dinosaur skeletons and dioramas showing how prehistoric people lived.

✳ *St. Louis, Missouri area:* The Devil's Bake Oven.
Cross the Mississippi River from St. Louis and drive south on Route 3 to Grand Tower, Illinois. Go to Grand Tower City Park, in the northwest of town, and look along the east bank of the Mississippi.

The marine fossils in this area are from 350 million years ago, when animals were first crawling onto land.

Indiana

✳ *Indianapolis:* Spergen Hill.
Take Interstate 65 south to highway 160 west. After about 15 miles (24 km) on 160, you will cross some railroad tracks. Immediately turn right onto a road with the sign: Harristown ¾ mile. Drive .7 mile (1.1 km), and park opposite the grocery store in Harristown. Walk back along the railroad tracks for about .3 mile (.5 km) to a railroad cut. Watch very carefully for trains!

A classic formation of snails and other fossils from the Paleozoic era.

✳ *Louisville, Kentucky Area:* Madison, Indiana.
Travel to Madison on Routes 42 and 421, and turn onto Route 7 north. Proceed .9 miles (1.4 km) and park in the small pull-off on the east side of the road.

The roadcut here has exposed brachiopods and other invertebrates from 450 million years ago.

Kansas

✳ *Kansas City area:* Holliday Road.
Take Interstate 245 south from Kansas 32, passing Topeka and crossing the Kansas River. Take the Holliday Road exit and park.

There is an exposure of Paleozoic rocks with many invertebrate fossils right next to the exit ramp.

Michigan

✳ *Detroit area:* The Grand Ledge ledges.
Go to the city of Grand Ledge, 11 miles west of Lansing on Michigan Route 43. Take East Jefferson Street along the south bank of the Grand River to Fitzgerald Park.

"The ledges" contain both plant and invertebrate fossils from the late Paleozoic era.

Nebraska

☞ *Harrison:* Agate Fossil Beds National Monument. Gering, NE 69341-0427. (308) 436-4340. Drive 23 miles south on Nebraska Route 29 from Harrison, or 34 miles north on 29 from Mitchell. The Park Road turns east off of 29, and runs three miles to park headquarters. The visitors center is open 9:00 A.M.–5:00 P.M. every day from May to September, and on weekends in the winter.

A 2-mile (3 km) trail leads to an exposure of fossils from 25 to 13 million years ago, showing what North America was like before humans arrived.

Ohio

✳ *Cincinnati area:* Waynesville Formation. Take Route 42 to Waynesville, Ohio. Park near the intersection with Route 73 (there's a traffic light here), at the base of the hill on Route 73's north side. Walk up about .4 miles (.6 km) to a rock outcrop.

Invertebrates from the early Paleozoic era, more than 400 million years ago, are lurking here.

☞ *Cleveland:* Cleveland Museum of Natural History. Wade Oval, University Circle, Cleveland, OH 44106. (216) 231-4600. Admission: $3.25 adults, $1.50 kids ages 7–17, $1.50 senior citizens and students with identification. Hours: Monday–Saturday, 10:00 A.M.–5:00 P.M.; Sunday, 10:00 A.M.–5:30 P.M.; from September to May the museum is open until 10:00 P.M. on Wednesday nights.

The paleontology collection contains unique dinosaur specimens like the skull of a *Nanotyrannosaur,* a pygmy version of *Tyrannosaurus,* and the skeleton of *Haplocanthosaurus,* a cousin of *Apatosaurus.*

Wisconsin

✳ *Milwaukee area:* Potosi Hill. Take highway 18 west to Fennimore, and turn south onto Route 61. Look for a roadcut about 3 miles (4.8 km) past the exit to Potosi, 1 mile (1.6 km) before crossing the Platte River. Stop and look at the roadcut on the east side of the highway.

The rocks exposed here contain marine invertebrate fossils from about 450 million years ago, before fish evolved.

SOUTH

Alabama

✳ *Mobile area:* St. Stephens Bluff. Drive to St. Stephens on Route 43 and highway 34. Go 2¼ miles (3.6 km) northeast to St. Stephens Bluff, on the west bank of the Tombigbee River. Look for the Lone Star Cement Quarry.

The quarry contains marine invertebrate fossils from the middle of the Cenozoic era.

Florida

✳ *Miami area:* Windley Key. Make arrangements to visit with the Miami Geological Society, P.O. Box 344156, Coral Gables, FL 33114. The site is along Route 1 south of Miami.

This fossil coral reef contains many marine invertebrates that lived in a community during the Ice Age.

Mississippi

✳ *Jackson:* Riverside Park. Take Lakeland Drive East exit off Interstate 55 in Jackson. Turn south on Highland Drive at the first traffic light. Proceed to the intersection with Riverside Drive and Riverside Park Circle. Take Riverside Park

Circle east and, after the circle turns north, park in the lot on the right. Walk northeast across the golf course to a small pond and a ravine.

The ravine holds marine invertebrate fossils from about 50 million years ago.

North Carolina

✳ *Wilmington area:* Waccamaw Formation.
Take highway 130 to about 2½ miles (4 km) northwest of Old Dock, North Carolina. Look for the marl pits the State Highway Department operates on both sides of the highway.

The banks and walls of these marl pits contain fossils from just before the Ice Age set in.

> On fossil expeditions, always bring along everything listed on page 16 — and an adult.

Texas

✳ *Houston area:* Stone City Bluff.
Go to Bryan, Texas. Take Texas highway 21 southwest to where it crosses the Brazos River. Look on the river's south bank.

This famous fossil-collecting site contains many invertebrate fossils from the early Cenozoic era.

✳ *Dallas area:* Hillsboro.
Take Interstate 35 south to Hillsboro. Then take Texas highway 171 northwest for about 5 miles (8 km), and look for an outcrop on the southwest side of the road.

This outcrop has abundant marine fossils from the late Mesozoic era.

Virginia

✳ *Richmond area:* St. Mary's Formation.
Drive on Route 10 to Claremont, Virginia. From the center of Claremont, take Route 609 south 1.1 miles (1.8 km), and turn left onto Route 1204. Drive .2 miles (.3 km), turn right onto a narrow dirt road, and follow it for about ¼ mile (.4 km) to the shore of the James River (Jamestown is just a few miles downstream). Walk along the shoreline northwest for about 50 yards (45 m).

The exposure of rocks here reveals fossils from the middle of the Cenozoic era.

NORTHEAST

Connecticut

☞ *New Haven:* Peabody Museum of Natural History.
170 Whitney Avenue, New Haven, CT 06520. (203) 432-5050. Admission: $2 adults, $1.50 senior citizens, $1 kids ages 5–15. Free on Tuesdays. Hours: Monday–Saturday, 9:00 A.M.–4:45 P.M.; Sundays and holidays, 1:00 P.M.–4:45 P.M.

The fossils assembled here include the famous dinosaurs *Allosaurus, Apatosaurus, Stegosaurus,* and *Triceratops.*

☞ *Hartford area:* Dinosaur State Park.
400 West Street, Rocky Hill, CT 06067. (203) 529-8423. Take Interstate 91 to Exit 23 and drive 1 mile (1.6 km) east, following the signs. Admission: $1 adults, $.50 kids. Hours: Tuesday–Sunday, 9:00 A.M.–4:30 P.M. Closed Mondays.

There are hundreds of dinosaur tracks preserved here. From April to November you can make casts of a dinosaur footprint to take home with you. You must bring the following materials: 10 pounds (4 kg) of plaster of Paris, ¼ cup (600 cc) of cooking oil, and some cloth rags. Other materials and instructions are available at the Park. Because the cast will take an hour to dry, you must arrive by 3:30 P.M. to start one.

Maryland

✳ Baltimore area: Chesapeake Bay cliffs.
Take Route 2 until it intersects with Governors Run Road (Route 509), south of Prince Frederick, Maryland. Drive to the end of Governors Run Road and park at the store called "The Cliffs." Pay $1.00 admission in the store (children under 12 free with parents), and walk about .3 mile (.5 km) north along the shore to the cliffs.

The fossils in these rocks come from the middle of the Cenozoic period, before the Ice Age.

Massachusetts

☞ *Boston area:* Museum of Comparative Zoology of Harvard University.
11 Divinity Avenue, Cambridge, MA 02138. (617) 495-1910. Admission: $2 adults, $.50 kids age 15 and under. Admission is free 9:00 A.M.–11:00 A.M. on Saturdays. Hours: Monday–Saturday, 9:00 A.M.–4:30 P.M., Sunday 1:00 P.M.–4:30 P.M..

This museum has North America's finest collection of reptile fossils from the early Mesozoic era, ancestors of all dinosaurs, birds, and mammals.

New York

☞ *New York, New York:* American Museum of Natural History.
79th Street at Central Park West, New York, NY 10024-5192. (212) 769-5100. Admission: Pay what you wish; free after 5:00 P.M. on Friday and Saturday. Hours: Sunday–Tuesday and Thursday, 10:00 A.M.–5:45 P.M.; Wednesday and Friday–Saturday, 10:00 A.M.–9:00 P.M. On school-visit days, kids under age 18 are not admitted without an adult until after 2:00 P.M.

The largest dinosaur collection in the world is found here, in the heart of New York City, along with exhibits on prehistoric humans, Ice Age mammals, and ancient invertebrates. This museum is our favorite, naturally.

✳ *Syracuse area:* Cazenovia.
Drive along Route 20 to about 2 miles (3.2 km) west of Cazenovia, New York, and look for a roadcut. Park and explore on either side of the road.

The fossils here are marine invertebrates from 370 millions years ago or so.

Be careful when you collect! Follow all the rules of fossil hunting on page 17.

Pennsylvania

✳ *New York area:* Stroudsburg, Pennsylvania.
Go east on Interstate 80 to Stroudsburg, Pennsylvania. Then drive north on Route 191 for about 4 miles (6.4 km). Park on the west side of the highway.

There are many invertebrates from the Paleozoic era here: trilobites, brachiopods, corals, and lots more.

✳ *Pittsburgh area:* Ames Formation.
Drive to Morgantown, West Virginia, by Interstate 79. Take Route 119 to the south of town. Park in the lot of the Morgantown Motel (ask for permission). Cross the street to the east side of the intersection, and climb about 35 feet (11 m) up the rock slope.

There will be a band of coal, about 1 foot (30 cm) thick, which was a swamp 250 million years ago. Just above the coal is a stripe of black shale which holds many good fossils.

☞ *Pittsburgh:* Carnegie Museum of Natural History.
4400 Forbes Avenue, Pittsburgh, PA 15213. (412) 622-6500. Admission: $5 adults, $3 students and kids ages 2–18. Hours: Tuesday–Sunday, 10:00 A.M.–6:00 P.M. Open until 9:00 P.M. on Friday. Closed Mondays.

The Carnegie Museum funded the exploration of what became Dinosaur National Monument, so it holds many great dinosaur fossils found on that expedition.

☞ *Philadelphia:* Academy of Natural Sciences.
19th and Benjamin Franklin Parkway, Philadelphia, PA 19103. (215) 299–1000. Admission: $4.50 adult, $3.50 kids ages 3–12. Hours: Monday–Friday, 10:00 A.M.–4:30 P.M.; Saturday–Sunday, 10:00 A.M.–5:00 P.M.

The dinosaur hall contains a *Hadrosaurus* fossil that was the first dinosaur discovered in the United States, and excellent exhibits on how the ancient animals lived.

Vermont

✳ *Burlington area:* Lake Champlain.
Take Routes 7 and 74 to Larrabees Point. Look for the landing of the ferry from Fort Ticonderoga. Just around the house from the landing, on the shore of Lake Champlain, is the fossil site.

Here you can find trilobites, brachiopods, bryozoans, and other fossils from about 450 million years ago.

Washington, D.C.

☞ *Washington, D.C.:* National Museum of Natural History.
Part of the Smithsonian Institution. Constitution Avenue, Washington, DC 20560. (202) 357-1300.

Hours: 10:00 A.M.–5:30 P.M. every day but Christmas, with extended evening hours in the summer.

The fossil halls lead you through "The History of Life," from the earliest fossils, past *Diplodocus*, under a pterosaur model, to the Ice Age. Don't miss the cast of a *Triceratops* skeleton out on the Mall.

CANADA

Alberta

✳ *Calgary area:* Dinosaur Trail around Drumheller, which is 1½ hours east of Calgary off Highway 1. This 30-mile (48 km) driving trail takes in two museums, one wildlife park, a canyon overlook, a river ferry (operating April–October), and some fine fossil-hunting ground.

☞ The Tyrell Museum of Paleontology.
is 4 miles (6 km) northwest of Drumheller on Highway 838, just over the Red Deer River in Midland Provincial Park. Box 7500, Drumheller, Alberta, Canada T0J 0Y0. (403) 823-7707. Hours: 9:00 A.M.–9:00 P.M. every day in the summer (Victoria Day weekend to Canadian Thanksgiving Day); Tuesday–Sunday, 10:00 A.M.–5:00 P.M. in the winter. Closed Mondays in the winter.

The Tyrell Museum displays over 200 dinosaur specimens and 35 complete skeletons, the most under one roof anywhere. There are also computer stations, hands-on exhibits, and a greenhouse of ancient plant species.

☞ Drumheller Dinosaur and Fossil Museum.
335 1st Street East, Drumheller, Alberta, Canada T0J 0Y0. (403) 823-2593. Admission: $1 adults, $.50 senior citizens and students ages 6–18. Hours: 10:00 A.M.–5:00 P.M. from May to October, with extended hours in July and August.

This small museum in the heart of Drumheller has on display a 30-foot (9 m) *Edmontosaurus* and the first *Pachyrhinosaurus* skull ever found.

☞ Dinosaur Provincial Park, Alberta, Canada.
The site of many fossil discoveries, this park is about
30 miles (48 km) north of Brooks, Alberta, spanning
the Red Deer River. It includes the Field Station of
the Tyrell Museum. Box 60, Patricia, Alberta, Canada
T0J 2K0. (403) 378-4342. Hours: 9:00 A.M.–9:00 P.M.
every day in the summer (Victoria Day weekend to
Thanksgiving Day); Saturday–Sunday, 10:00 A.M.–
5:00 P.M. in the winter. Closed weekdays in the winter.

    The Field Station has dinosaur fossils and models
on display, a small film theater, and a lab where you
can watch paleontologists at work. In addition, the
park contains a scenic campground and trails.

Ontario

☞ *Ottawa:* National Museum of Natural Sciences.
Victoria Memorial Museum, Metcalfe and McCloud
Streets, Ottawa, Ontario, Canada K1P 6P4. (613) 996-
3102: Admission: $2 adults, $1.50 senior citizens and
students, $1 kids age 6–16, $5 family rate. Admission
on Thursdays is free. Hours: Friday–Wednesday,
10:00 A.M.–5:00 P.M.; Thursday, 10:00 A.M.–8:00 P.M.
The museum opens at 9:30 A.M. from May through
August.

    Fossils of whales and seals that swam in the
waters over Ontario during the late Ice Age are on
display, as well as dinosaur skeletons from Western
Canada.

Index

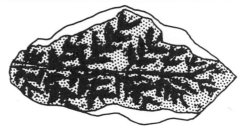

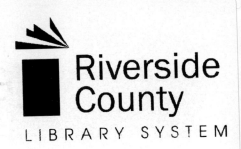